PHANTOM THIEF RED

**A Brand-New Heist
for a Brand-New Red!**

Shin Akigi

ILLUSTRATION BY Shu

New York

PHANTOM THIEF RED

Translation by Winifred Bird ☆ Cover art by Shu

Shin Akigi

This book is a work of fiction. Names, characters, places, and incidents are the product of the author's imagination or are used fictitiously. Any resemblance to actual events, locales, or persons, living or dead, is coincidental.

KAITO RED Vol.1 NIDAIME KAITO, DEBUT SURU ☆ NO MAKI
©Shin Akigi 2010 ©Shu 2010
First published in Japan in 2010 by KADOKAWA CORPORATION, Tokyo.
English translation rights arranged with KADOKAWA CORPORATION, Tokyo through TUTTLE-MORI AGENCY, INC., Tokyo.

English translation © 2023 by Yen Press, LLC

JY
150 West 30th Street, 19th Floor
New York, NY 10001

Visit us at jyforkids.com • facebook.com/jyforkids • twitter.com/jyforkids
jyforkids-blog.tumblr.com • instagram.com/jyforkids

First JY Edition: November 2023
Edited by Yen On Editorial: Anna Powers
Designed by Yen Press Design: Eddy Mingki

JY is an imprint of Yen Press, LLC.
The JY name and logo are trademarks of Yen Press, LLC.

The publisher is not responsible for websites (or their content) that are not owned by the publisher.

Library of Congress Cataloging-in-Publication Data
Names: Akigi, Shin, author. | Shu (Illustrator), illustrator. | Bird, Winifred, translator.
Title: Phantom thief red / Shin Akigi ; illustration by Shu ; translated by Winifred Bird.
Other titles: Kaito red. English
Description: First Yen On edition. | New York : Yen On, 2023- | Contents: A brand-new heist for a brand-new Red! — | Audience: Ages 8-12 | Audience: Grades 4-6
Identifiers: LCCN 2023031036 | ISBN 9781975378103 (v. 1 ; trade paperback) | ISBN 9781975378127 (v. 2 ; trade paperback) | ISBN 9781975378141 (v. 3 ; trade paperback) | ISBN 9781975378165 (v. 4 ; trade paperback) | ISBN 9781975378189 (v. 5 ; trade paperback) | ISBN 9781975378202 (v. 6 ; trade paperback)
Subjects: LCGFT: Light novels.
Classification: LCC AE3 .W32 2023 | DDC [Fic]—dc23
LC record available at https://lccn.loc.gov/2023031036

ISBNs: 978-1-9753-7810-3 (paperback)
        978-1-9753-7811-0 (ebook)

10 9 8 7 6 5 4 3 2 1

LBK

Printed in the United States of America

PHANTOM THIEF RED

**A Brand-New Heist
for a Brand-New Red!**

Table of Contents

Asuka Kouzuki

Twelve years old, about to start junior high. Second-generation Phantom Thief Red, super athletic, in charge of carrying out plans. Cheerful and energetic, doesn't sweat the details.

Kei Kouzuki

Asuka's cousin, also twelve. Rarely talks, is mean when he does. Computer genius, in charge of strategy and guidance.

Tsubasa Kouzuki

Asuka's father, first-generation Phantom Thief Red. Big, burly, whiz-bang dad.

Keiichiro Kouzuki

Kei's father. Quiet like Kei, except when he's working as the Phantom Thief…!

Misaki Himuro

Asuka's best friend. Says what she thinks, grew up with Asuka and understands her.

Prologue

It was spring vacation of sixth grade—the end of March, one week before Asuka (say it like "Aska") Kouzuki would officially start junior high. Oh, and Asuka is me!

I was free from homework for now, so I was being as lazy as humanly possible. How lazy? Let's just say I reread almost every manga in the house. All one hundred or so of them.

"Guess this is it." I sighed.

I was partway through the very last volume when my dad called to me from the hallway.

"Hey, Asuka! Can I talk to you?"

"What about?" I answered without looking up.

"Can you come to my room? I've got something to tell you."

"Does it have to be now?"

I still had about half the volume left. The main character was in trouble, and I was dying to know what happened.

"It's important," Dad said.

I looked up. Important? What was such a big deal? I tried to think of something, but...

…Oh. Maybe he was finally getting married again.

My mom passed away in a car accident when I was little, and it was hard to imagine anyone else wanting to marry *my* dad.

Reluctantly, I tore myself away from the manga and stood up.

"Hold on a sec! I'm on my way."

I opened the door, and Dad was standing there.

I'm pretty tall for my age, but Dad's so tall that I have to lean back to look him in the face. He's almost six feet, built like an athlete, and not a bad-looking guy, either—although I know I'm biased. You'd think the ladies would be lining up to date him, except his fashion sense is a disaster. He'll go outside in literally anything.

Take right now, for instance. He'd just thrown on an old, stretched-out shirt like it didn't even matter. I've talked to him about it a million times, but he still just takes whatever's on top of the pile in his dresser and wears it.

How is this guy ever going to convince someone to marry him?

"What? Why are you staring at me?" he asked.

"Nothing. What did you want to talk about?" I asked.

"I'll tell you when we get to my room. They're both waiting for us."

"Who? Uncle K and Kei?"

"Yeah."

Dad's room is Japanese style, like mine, with tatami mats.

When we walked in, the low table he always uses was set up in the middle. Uncle K—Keiichiro, that is—was sitting on the far side. He's lanky and wears glasses, and his face looked as kind as it did the last time I saw him.

My cousin Kei, who's the same age as me, was sitting on the other side of the table. He's never shown much emotion, even as a little kid. His face is like a mask, and he's really pale. Plus, he never cuts his hair, so his bangs cover about half of it.

The two of them had been at our place all morning, but I'd only seen them at lunch. Even though Kei's my cousin, Dad and I only meet up with him occasionally, and I've hardly talked to him at all. He's as antisocial as he looks, and I've never felt the urge to make conversation.

Dad sat down next to his brother, so I sat down next to my cousin. I looked over at Kei, but he seemed totally uninterested in me. Then Dad coughed to get my attention again.

Right. What the heck did he want to talk about? It must be super important if he'd invited the relatives.

"Asuka, have you heard of Phantom Thief Red?"

Huh? That was random.

I cocked my head. He brought the three of us here to talk about Phantom Thief Red?

"Of course, but…," I answered, confused.

Phantom Thief Red is, as the name implies, a robber. But not an ordinary robber. Red could sneak into any place in Japan, even the most closely guarded, and never get caught.

And last (but definitely not least), Red only steals from bad guys!

Red's a fearless phantom thief, just like Lupin and Kid.

The only difference is, Red isn't a character in a manga or a book. Red is real.

A real live phantom thief. Not that I'd met them or anything.

Since Red seems to be one of the good guys, they're always making the front page on the local newspapers and trending on the internet…or so I've heard. I don't use the internet, and the only part of the paper I read is the TV listings. Everything I just said about Red, I heard from my friend Misaki.

"Oh, good," Dad went on. "I figured you might not have heard of them since you don't read the paper."

"I do too read the paper!"

Y'know, just the part about what's on TV.

"Sorry, my bad. Kei, I assume you've heard of Red?"

"Yeah…," Kei said.

He sounded sleepy. Wonder if he stayed up late. I saw him holding back a yawn a second ago.

Dad stopped talking and threw Uncle K a glance.

What did that mean?

"I'm going to tell you something, and I want the two of you to stay calm," Dad said.

He was so serious about this that I was starting to get nervous.

"The truth is…"

"Uh-huh?" I sat very still.

"…Phantom Thief Red is me and Uncle Keiichiro."

Wait, what?

What did he just say? Phantom who is what…??

"H-h-hey, Dad, at least smile if you're gonna make a crazy joke!"

You can't just string us along with that buildup—it's not fair!

"…I'm not joking, Asuka. Although, I can see why you'd think I was," he said calmly, after a pause.

Dad's always kidding around, but Uncle K is more the quiet type. I couldn't really see him getting in on a prank this elaborate.

…So was it true?

Dad and Uncle K were Phantom Thief Red?

My mouth dropped open.

Now that I thought about it, Dad did tend to disappear on "work trips" for days at a time, even though he was a cook at an Italian restaurant. It was a little fishy.

Were those trips what I was thinking they were?

I looked over at Kei, hoping he'd save me. Not that I would normally want to ask for his help, but I was running out of options.

He didn't look any friendlier than a minute ago.

"Okay, let's say it's true—so what? Why are you telling us this?" Kei asked.

He was infuriatingly calm. Still, I was glad at least one of us was.

"Y-yeah! Even if you guys are Phantom Thief Red—and that's a big if—why are you telling us your secret?"

Dad smiled and nodded, like he thought that was a great question.

"Because starting tomorrow, the two of you are going to be Phantom Thief Red."

Tomorrow, we're going to be... Huh?

It took a good ten seconds for that to sink in.

"*What?* Wait a second! What are you talking about?!" I asked, leaning over the table. I glanced at Kei. Even he looked surprised.

"We never told you this, but our family have been phantom thieves for generations. There are rumors the Rat Brat was one of our ancestors."

"The Rat Brat?"

We have rodents in the family?

I glanced at Kei—maybe he would know what the heck Dad was talking about. His dull eyes were now wide-open and bright with interest.

"Jirokichi was known as the Rat Brat," he explained calmly. "He was one of the great thieves of the Edo days, a couple hundred years back. People say he robbed more than a hundred samurai houses and stole more than ten thousand *ryo*. That'd be worth millions today. They say he was like Robin Hood, robbing the rich to give to the poor."

Kei sure knows a lot about old-timey thieves.

"Of course, I just heard the stories about our ancestors from Granddad," Dad went on. "I don't know if it's true. But it *is* true that most people in our family are phantom thieves. And when children turn thirteen, tradition says they have to join the family business."

"This is all so sudden…and I'm still only twelve," I said.

"You're turning thirteen this year, aren't you?" Dad countered.

Yeah, but shouldn't we do it right?

"Oh, and if you are going to take up the mantle, can you keep the name *Phantom Thief Red*? Your uncle and I came up with that. Once you're all settled, we're officially retiring."

"Hold on now, this isn't about whether we take on your name or when you get to retire! Ugh, my head's a mess!"

"Yes, it's hardly a logical argument," Kei pointed out. "Anyway, even if *I* can do it…"

He glanced at me.

What's that supposed to mean? That I'm not phantom thief material?

I was about to complain, but then I realized it might be better not to work in the thief business and shut my mouth.

"She'll be fine, Kei," Dad said. He sounded awfully confident. "Asuka, how high can you climb on the outside of a building without using rope?"

"A building? Um…to the seventeenth story. No, wait, I think I can get to the twentieth now."

Uncle K and Kei stared at me. What, was that weird?

"…Tsuba, what crazy things have you been teaching your daughter?" Uncle K asked Dad, then sighed.

"What? Climbing walls is a necessary skill!" Dad answered.

"You're not wrong…"

"W-w-wait one second!" I interrupted.

Uncle K seemed convinced, but I was not.

"Were you training me for this without even telling me?"

When I thought back on it, I realized he'd been doing this stuff since I was little. He'd had me running 10Ks every morning, climbing walls, getting out of rope ties, and picking locks. He taught me plenty of other things a normal dad wouldn't teach his daughter, too. I'd always known we were a little different from other people. But I never dreamed he was training me in the art of breaking and entering!

"I guess you could say that, but thanks to me, you'll be able to take over as Phantom Thief Red starting tomorrow without a hitch! No complaints, right?"

"Wrong!" I shouted back.

"Oh, calm down. Anyway, what about you, Kei? Don't you want to give it a try?" Dad asked, ignoring me.

I assumed he would say no, but he just nodded.

"I'm willing to do it."

"Wait, what? Really?" I asked. I couldn't believe my ears.

"If it's been the family business for generations, I can't really avoid it."

Come on, don't you have a spine?

"So it's just 'cause you can't avoid it? Don't you think he should be a little more enthusiastic, Dad?"

"Nah, he's fine."

But, but…

"What about you, Asuka? Do you not want to do it?"

"M-m-me?" I hesitated. "Um, well, I wouldn't say I'm *not* interested, but…"

I was surprised at first, but that didn't mean I wanted to give a hard no. And Phantom Thief Red didn't seem like a villain.

"Great! So it's decided!" Dad said, slapping his knee.

"Hey, I didn't say yes yet…"

"Now that you've agreed, we'd better find you some work. Something fitting for your debut. Keiichi?"

"…All right. Give me two or three days."

"Hear that? For now, we'll give you the assignments—who to rob and what to take. Oh, and one more thing, Asuka."

"…What?" I asked. It was no use arguing anymore.

"Starting today, your uncle and cousin are going to live with us. Be nice to them, okay?"

"Thank you for sharing your home with us, Asuka," Uncle K said, smiling.

Live with us? Both of them?

"Whaaaaaat?!"

And that was how Kei and I became Phantom Thief Red.

1

Roommate Worries

The next morning, I woke up bright-eyed and bushy-tailed.

Starting today, I was Phantom Thief Red.

I was a little miffed about the decision being made for me. But just thinking about being Red made me excited, or maybe nervous, or…whatever it was that was making my heart race.

I got dressed and went to the living room.

"Morning!"

"Oh, Asuka, you're up!"

With an apron tied over his broad shoulders, Dad seemed extremely energetic for this hour.

"Mmm, that smells great," I said.

Miso soup, steamed rice, *tamagoyaki* omelets, homemade potato salad, and mini hotdogs were set on the table.

Dad sure knows how to make a breakfast! It looked delicious, as always.

But where were Uncle K and Kei?

I looked around and found the two of them sitting at the dining table, staring into space like zombies.

"Good morning, Uncle K."

"……Huh? Oh, Asuka… Morning…"

Was he even awake yet? Kei didn't look any better, either. *I should leave them alone for now.*

"Thanks for cooking, Dad! So what's the plan for today?" I asked, digging into breakfast.

Nothing boring about this spring break!

Uncle K and Kei started sluggishly putting food in their mouths and glumly chewing it. Were they finally waking up?

"Well, for starters, you can help these two move in."

"But what about the assignment for Red?"

"That comes after unpacking," Dad said, like that was obvious. I slumped in my chair. *Disappointed* would be putting it mildly.

And after all my excitement over phantom thieving. Why'd I even bother getting nervous?

"Are you serious?" I asked, glaring at Dad.

Uncle K and Kei's boxes had just arrived. There were surprisingly few of them, but both father and son were carrying their computers as carefully as if they were newborn babies. What a weird family.

I was glad there weren't many boxes to move, but there was another big problem…

"Our place is small," Dad said, shrugging. "These things happen."

"But I don't want to share my room with Kei. I'm twelve, you know!!"

Dad was right. The only rooms in the house were my room, Dad's room, and the living room. The two of them had slept in the living room the night before, but they couldn't do that forever. Dad had suggested that Uncle K move into his room and Kei move into my room. I was not happy about it.

"I could share your room instead," Dad suggested.

"Nope. No way."

"…"

Oops. He looked hurt. Guess I shouldn't have answered so quickly. Honestly, though, I like Dad, but having him as a roommate is a whole other story.

"Your daughter just rejected you," Uncle K said, laughing.

"…She's been so mean to me lately. My daughter's almost a bona fide teenager now…," Dad said, his shoulders drooping.

He was being melodramatic, if you ask me. Anyway, he shouldn't be saying that stuff right in front of me!

"Dad, you're so embarrassing. Let's just move this."

I grabbed one end of the bed that was in the living room. There wasn't space in my room for two beds, so Dad had bought a bunk bed from a thrift store in the shopping arcade.

"…You got that? It's pretty heavy. I can take your end," Uncle K offered, looking worried.

"Oh, this is nothing," I said.

"Asuka's in great shape. Look," Dad said, picking the other end up off the ground.

"Almost seventy pounds, you think?" I said.

"Just about. I can do this with one hand."

He readjusted his grip and pumped the bed up and down with his left hand.

"Hey, stop shaking it around!" I complained.

"Sorry." He brought it back parallel with the floor.

"…Tsuba…exactly what kind of training did you put your daughter through?" Uncle K pressed his hand to his forehead.

"Oh, you know… The usual," Dad said, shaking his head—although he was getting a shifty look in his eyes.

Once we carried the bed carefully into my room, we brought in the top level and set it on the base. We screwed it in place, and voilà.

"Not too shabby, eh? You each have a desk, too. It's starting to look like a room for two," Dad said.

"Only because you forced it to be," I reminded him.

"Don't say that. I'll let you order whatever you want at my restaurant."

"For real?!"

The Italian restaurant where Dad works is famous (at least

around here) for its reasonable prices and good food. A magazine once even did a feature on his wood-fired pizzas.

"Then I guess I forgive you. I've always wanted to see how many slices of pizza I could eat."

"Now, now…let's not get carried away," Dad said with an awkward smile.

Aw, come on! I could only eat, like, ten max.

"So, you decide who's taking the top bunk yet?" he asked, surveying our handiwork with the bed.

It was a very important question, after all.

"I'd rather be on top. What about you, Kei?" I asked my cousin, who was off in a corner.

"I don't care."

Figures. That's about what I expected.

"Okay," I said, "then I'll take the top, and you be on the bottom."

"All right. Oh, and…"

"What?" I turned back around.

Kei's hair was mostly covering his eyes, but I could tell he was looking at me. His expression was so blank, though, that I had no idea what he might say.

"…I'll try to stay out of the room as much as possible. I don't want to get in your way."

With that, he slipped past Dad and out the door.

A minute later, I heard the front door close.

Oops.

Was that my fault?

"Uh-oh. So much for teamwork. You two gonna be okay?" Dad asked jokingly.

"B-but...I didn't expect him to do *that*."

I never thought Kei was the overly sensitive type.

"Well, that's one reason we're having you share a room. Good communication with your partner is key in this job... so try to make it work, okay?" Dad said, patting my head before he left the room.

Was that the issue?

I wondered if I could really get along with Kei.

On the other hand, I was excited about my new work as Red.

I guess Dad and Uncle K really put one over on me.

2

Seriously? This Is Our First Assignment?!

"Ugh, I'm bored…"

I was lying on the top bunk in my room. The ceiling was a lot closer than it used to be, but I could survey the whole room from up here. Since I liked high places, it wasn't all that bad.

Kei was typing away on the laptop on his desk, which we'd carried into the room.

Taptaptaptaptaptaptaptap…

He was typing so fast, I could barely follow his fingers with my eyes. I'm surprised he doesn't get cramps.

When he slipped out the previous day, I didn't know what to do, but he came back last night acting totally normal. I guess that means he wasn't mad? I don't get him.

"Hey, Kei? Have you heard anything from our dads?"

"…About what?"

"About Phantom Thief Red, obviously. We're taking up the mantle now, right? But we haven't stolen anything or made any plans or even done any training!"

"Our dads will probably give us an assignment soon."

He didn't sound very interested, and his fingers didn't even slow down once. Wonder what it's like inside his head.

"You're really having fun with that computer, huh?" I asked, taking a sudden interest.

He'd been on his computer until late last night, too. Guess they're more interesting than I thought.

"Computers aren't fun or not fun. They're just tools. It all depends on how you use them."

That was a very long answer for him. Maybe computers are one of the few things he actually will talk about a little.

"You can play games on them, right?"

"If you have the right software installed."

"Huh."

I nodded, but I had no idea what he meant. "Install"? What, like a horse? Oh well, whatever. I can figure it out if I ever need to.

"Geez, I'm so bored. Maybe I'll go talk to Dad."

I sat up—carefully, so I wouldn't bang my head on the ceiling—and jumped down from the bed. I landed noiselessly on the tatami mat.

"…What are you, a cat?" Kei muttered, and his typing actually stopped.

"That was nothing. Anyway, come with me."

"Why?"

He didn't let it show, but I knew he didn't want to. The way he said it made it seem like I was dragging him somewhere…which I guess I was.

"Just stand up, okay?"

I put my hands under his armpits and pulled up... Whoa, he sure was light! Maybe even lighter than me! I'm like four inches taller than him, but geez...

"You gonna put me down anytime soon?" He glared at me, suspended from my hands.

"Sorry!" I hurriedly dropped him.

Once he was back on his own feet, he rolled his neck.

"Sore shoulders? You look like an old man!" I commented.

"Shoulders can hurt at any age."

Uh...that's not the point.

"Anyway...let's go," he said.

Dad was in his room. He was lying on the tatami, staring at the ceiling. Like a lion in its pen at the zoo. Since the restaurant was closed for the day, he'd probably lay there all day if I let him.

"Hey, Dad, could you sit up? It's embarrassing."

I decided not to tell him I'd just left my own bed about five minutes earlier.

"Oh, hi, Asuka. And Kei. What's up?"

Still flat on his back, he tilted his head to look at me upside down. Would we be standing on our heads to him, then?

"You know what's up," I replied. "I'm so bored! Isn't there something we can steal?"

"Hey now, don't say that. If you go around swiping random people's stuff, you're just a regular old thief."

"But we *are* thieves."

"Oh, no, Phantom Thief Red is no common criminal. Red is the friend of the weak and the enemy of evil. And Red always returns stolen goods to their rightful owner."

I think he was trying to give a swashbuckling speech, but when the swashbuckler is lying on his back like a wet rag…

"Uncle Tsuba, I want to talk about something," Kei said, suddenly standing next to me instead of behind my back.

"Sure, what?"

"I did a little research on Red."

He wasn't mumbling like usual. So he could talk normally! He should try that more often.

"You did, eh? And did you learn anything?"

Dad was smiling at Kei.

"Last month, a group of con artists was wiped out," said Kei. "Three months ago, a bunch of people were rescued from would-be slavers overseas, and the criminals were discovered tied up on the boat. There are more examples all around the country...and the world. Red was behind every one of them."

"Wait, Red did all that?" I interrupted. That sounded more like a superhero!

"According to what I read, Phantom Thief Red's calling card was left behind each time. And my dad was always out when those incidents happened."

So that's what Kei wanted to look into. He sure is skeptical for someone who acts so apathetic—although I have to admit, it's hard to imagine Dad and Uncle K as Red.

"Not bad for just reading the news report," Dad said. "But did you hear about this one? Your father and I stole back some artwork that a ring of thieves took from the Louvre in France!"

I know about the Louvre—that's where the *Mona Lisa* is. "I never heard about that. Have you, Kei?"

He thought for a second, then said, "...If I remember correctly, a famous ring of thieves was arrested three years ago for robbing the Louvre. The odd thing was, not a single painting went missing from the museum."

"How? Did they make some kind of mistake?" I asked.

"Nope. The security cameras showed multiple paintings

being stolen, so there's no question they were taken," Kei said.

"Of course not. We put them back a couple hours after the ring of thieves took them. And while we were at it, we dropped off the criminals and the evidence with the police," Dad said, like that was the obvious thing to do.

Seriously, what's wrong with them?

"Then everything makes sense," Kei said. "Apparently, the thieves told the police a 'red devil' had come, but the police didn't take them seriously. I suspect…that must have been Phantom Thief Red."

Kei didn't say anything else, so I assumed that meant he was satisfied.

But what did Dad and Uncle K do to get called a devil?

"We just had a little fun," said Dad. "Maybe too much fun, which is why we didn't leave a card. Even now, I don't think many people realize Red was behind that one."

Really? This is a big deal; why are you grinning?

"Geez, Dad, I bet even one of those famous paintings could have gotten us out of this dinky apartment and into a fancy condo," I mumbled.

"We're not doing this for money," Dad answered proudly. He tried to puff out his chest and everything, but he was still lying on the tatami, so it didn't quite work.

"Yeah, yeah. Tell me that when we don't have to bargain with the guy at the fish stall and the produce lady anymore. Anyway, you really don't have a job for us?"

"Let's see… Aha! This might do." Dad pulled two folded pieces of notepaper from his pocket and passed them to me.

"What's this?" I opened the slips and read them out loud.

"Daikon radish, konjac jelly, fish cakes… Hey! This is a shopping list!"

"It sure is. We're having *oden* stew tonight, kids!"

"Why do you think that's exciting? Anyway, it's almost April!"

"Picky, picky. *Oden*'s not just for winter."

Uh…yes, it is.

"You can show Kei around the neighborhood while you're at it. When you get back, I'll give you a real assignment."

"You will, huh?"

"Well, not if you keep treating me like a liar!"

There he goes again. He's a total kid sometimes…

"Fine. Kei, let's go."

I glanced over my shoulder, and Kei sighed and followed me. He always silently does what he's told.

"I think I'll give you the shopping money, Kei," Dad said, handing over our errand wallet.

"Hey, why not me?" I protested.

"Because you'd probably come back with cookies or something."

Urk. He knows me all too well. I was definitely planning to pick up some cookies while we were out—but that didn't make it any less annoying.

"Fine, fine," I answered. "You don't trust me; I get it. Then

I don't care about you. Let's go, Kei." I turned my back on him and marched out of the room.

"Hey, wait! Asuka! I never said I didn't trust you…"

I tried not to smile as Dad's anxious voice drifted over my shoulder. Maybe that was a mean thing to say, but recently, he'd been giving me a hard time.

Kei trailed after me silently as we left the apartment and stepped into the hallway outside. He was surprisingly obedient…or maybe just too lazy to resist. That was the vibe I was getting from his expression.

Meanwhile, I could still hear Dad wailing. "Asukaaaa!"

"Is he okay?" Kei asked, stopping to look back at the door.

"Uh…"

Did I go too far?

"…I'll check in with him later," I said.

"Okay," Kei replied, nodding and starting to walk again.

Was he worried about us? Hard to believe.

We took the stairs down instead of the elevator. We live in apartment 503 in building B, so we're on the fifth floor. Kei made a face when I skipped the elevator, but it's just five flights.

"Hey, look. I made that hole," I said, pointing out the inch-wide hole in the wall with the banister on the third-floor landing. Kei gave me a suspicious look. "During training, I was about to jump down to the ground from there, but the old mailman decided to come by right then and stop me. But then he fell over, and his motorbike helmet banged into the corner there, and the concrete broke off."

"…"

Kei glared at me.

Come on, it wasn't my fault!

"Blame Dad; he made me do it! Anyway, I was still in preschool. Look at me now!"

I put one hand on top of the wall and vaulted over. I felt my body soaring through the air and my hair dancing in the wind.

"Ta-daa!"

Twirling around, I nailed the landing. It was only about a thirty-foot jump. Easy-peasy.

"No problem, right?" I called up to him.

Kei narrowed his eyes and sighed. "I don't think I should consider you a normal human being," he said.

"What's that supposed to mean?"

What else would I be? An endangered animal?

But I guess I am kinda weird. I've never really thought about it before.

It's all Dad's fault. Geez!

3

Is Kei Actually a Genius?

We left our apartment building, crossed the parking lot and the little grassy park in the complex, and came out onto the road. About fifty yards down the road was a residential neighborhood, and past that was the shopping arcade, a long street lined with shops that was covered by a roof. Inside, you could buy produce, fish, clothes, flowers, Chinese food, and various other things each at their own little shop.

"This is our neighborhood shopping area. You can get most stuff here," I told Kei.

He peered around like he'd never seen a shopping arcade before. Maybe he doesn't usually get to do this kind of thing.

"Oh, hello, Asuka. Running an errand for your father?" the fish guy asked as we passed. He always wore the same blue rubber apron and smelled like the sea.

"Yup. Sorry to tell you we're having *oden* today."

"Say it ain't so! …Hey, is that kid behind you with you?"

"Yeah, he's my cousin Kei. He just moved in with us, so you might be seeing him around."

Kei bowed his head silently. Wish he was a little friendlier.

On the other hand, if he was like, "Hiya!" I might pass out from shock.

I said good-bye to the fish guy and kept walking.

"We just passed a produce stall. You're not going to buy anything?" Kei asked.

"No, we've got a lot to get today, so I figured we'd go to the supermarket. Easier, right?"

"Oh, I guess that makes sense…"

He genuinely may have never been shopping before. The more I learn about this guy, the weirder he gets.

"Here's the supermarket," I said.

It was on the far side of the shopping arcade, next to the train station, with a sign featuring the company's trademark green leaf. When Kei and I stepped inside, the store was a little crowded. Well, it was the afternoon.

"You carry the basket," I told him.

"What basket?" He cocked his head.

"…Have you seriously never been to a supermarket before?"

"Not in the past few years."

"What do you guys eat?"

"Bentos from the convenience store and stuff from the deli. Dad can't cook…"

True enough, I couldn't remember ever seeing Uncle K cook.

"No wonder you never have any energy. Breakfast is the most important meal of the day!"

"I take vitamins."

That's not the point! The point is, it's important to eat tasty food. My dad can cook anything, so I never have to worry about that.

By the way, Kei's mom passed away, too. When he and I were little, our moms went on a trip together overseas and got in a car accident.

Come to think of it, that's when Kei and I kinda stopped talking to each other. Maybe it was because it reminded us too much of our moms. Although these days, it's the opposite—I wish I could remember her more.

"Why are you spacing out?" Kei asked, scrunching his eyebrows at me.

"No reason. Anyway, let's get this done. First, we need daikon for 98 yen."

Looking at my list, I tossed one long white radish into the basket.

"Next, two blocks of konjac for 205 yen, one pack of fish cakes for twenty percent off 210, one pack of tofu balls for ten percent off 148, oh, and of course, we need the other kind of fish cake. Two of those for 218. Hey, look, the deep-fried tofu is on sale for 88! Lucky me, I'll buy two. *Shirataki* noodles for 98, eggs for 188, kelp for 298… Boy, that sure is expensive."

I tossed everything into the basket. Soon, it was filled to the top. Kei switched from carrying it with one hand to two.

How could I rely on him if he thought *that* was heavy?

"You okay?" I asked.

"Um, yeah," he answered.

He didn't look okay. But if he wasn't gonna admit it, I'd let him power through.

"Right. Two boxes of aluminum foil for 598, a soap refill for 288, garbage bags for 498, pickled daikon for 128, ketchup for 178, and a can of tuna for 412. Ooh, strawberries are forty percent off 398. Let's get two! Noodle sauce for 199, miso for ten percent off 248, chocolate cookies for 211 yen, and curry roux for two for 338 yen."

"Hey, one of those wasn't on the list, was it?"

Busted.

"Who cares about a few little cookies? We deserve pay for doing errands."

"Uncle Tsuba didn't give us permission."

I swear, this kid. I reluctantly returned the package of cookies to the shelf.

"Let's see, is that everything?" I asked.

"Definitely," he said, nodding vigorously.

Wait a second...did I ever show him the list?

"How do you know?" I asked. "You didn't check the list, did you?"

"I saw it when I took the purse from your dad."

"You mean you memorized it after one glance?!"

He couldn't have caught it for more than a few seconds.

"I only need one glance to memorize something that short," he said, like that was normal.

And he was treating *me* like a rare animal!

"We have everything, so let's go pay," he said, walking toward the register.

"Hey, wait!" I said, trailing after him.

There were lines at all the registers, so we joined the shortest one.

"Hold the basket, okay?" he asked.

"Sure, why? Too heavy for ya?"

"No," he said, taking the purse from his pocket. Without pausing, he pulled out one five-thousand-yen bill and eight coins.

"But we don't know the total yet," I said.

"I do. I calculated it already."

He did? But there were discounts, and we were talking!

"So how much is it?" I asked.

"4,921 yen."

He sounded super confident—or maybe more surprised that I *didn't* know.

The person ahead of us finished at the register, and it was our turn. I put the basket on the counter.

"Hello," said the lady at the cash register. Before she could finish, Kei put the money down, too.

She raised an eyebrow at him before starting to scan the food. As the scanner beeped, the machine added up the prices.

"…That will be 4,921 yen," she said.

On the nose!

Did he really add it all in his head?

The checkout lady counted the money and glanced at Kei with surprise. *Me, too, checkout lady.* Mental math with discounts is complicated. I'd probably give up after three items.

Kei took the receipt calmly. Was he a child prodigy or something?

At the very least, he was more than your average anti-social kid.

When we got home, Dad was pacing back and forth in the living room. Isn't that what stressed-out bears at the zoo do?

"What are you doing, Dad?"

"Oh, Asuka, you came back!"

"Of course I did. I just went to get groceries."

"But you were angry when you left. I thought you'd stay out for a while…"

Oh yeah. I was so surprised about Kei, I'd forgotten our argument.

"Sorry. I wasn't mad," I said.

"Really? Well, that's good…"

Dad is a real drill sergeant when I'm training, but otherwise, he's a softy. Even for me, his daughter, this difference can be hard to deal with.

"Anyway, we got all the groceries, so now can we have our assignment?" I asked, holding out my hand to him.

"Sure. Here it is."

He placed two folded pieces of paper—bigger than the ones with the shopping list—in my palm.

"It's written on here?" I asked.

This time is for real, I thought as I unfolded the paper.

It said, *Please call me if you find my cat Mita. My phone number is…*

There was a photo of a brown cat on the top half of the paper. I didn't recognize it, but it looked smug and pampered, and who calls their cat Mita anyway…? *Wait a second!*

"H-hey, Asuka, are you okay? You're turning red. Do you have a fever?"

"No, I'm angry! What is the meaning of this? You gave me a lost-cat flyer!!"

"I want you to find the cat."

"What kind of assignment is that?!" I glared at him. This had to be some kind of joke.

"D-don't take this the wrong way, but, well, how can you do Red's work if you can't even find a cat? Think of it as a warm-up," he said.

A warm-up, huh? He wasn't trying to double-cross me, was he?

"After you do this," he continued, "I'll give you a certified robbery job."

"Promise?"

"Promise. Have I ever lied to you?"

"You didn't tell me about Red."

"Ouch. I guess you have a point…," he mumbled, looking away.

"All right, I'll hunt down the cat. But this is your last chance," I said.

I looked back at Kei. His face was nearly blank, but I deduced he was thinking, *I guess I should go with you.*

Was I starting to learn to read his expressions?

Were we starting to work together as Red?

4

Asuka Battles the Cat!

The first place we went was the park, which is in the opposite direction from the shopping arcade. It was full of lower-elementary-aged kids running around.

"I don't think it's here," I said.

We'd gone all around the park searching for the cat, but it was nowhere to be seen.

"...Based on the picture, I think it's a Scottish fold," said Kei, who was walking next to me.

"A Scottie?"

Wasn't that a kind of dog?

"No, a Scottish fold cat. It's a mutated variant that was discovered in 1961 in Scotland. Their ears are folded over, and they have short fur."

I looked at the flyer again.

"Oh, you're right! Its ears are folded. But why do you know that? Are you a cat person?"

"No. I hate animals."

He was wrinkling his nose and everything. Wow, the

hatred was real. So why did he know so much about them? He's so weird.

"Any ideas for how to find it?" I asked.

"Cats are nocturnal, so it probably spends the day sleeping in some high, warm spot."

"I've heard cats like warm spots, but why up high?"

"Safety. Cats evolved to live in the forest, and they think treetops and places like that are safe. Rooftops are ideal for them. They're warm from the sun, and they don't have to worry about being attacked."

"Interesting."

He knew an awful lot for someone who hated animals. Not only was he insanely fast at math, but he was also full of information. New nickname: the human encyclopedia.

"See ya," he said, turning his back on me and starting toward the park exit.

"Hey, wait! Where are you going?" I shouted.

"This is a job for Red, right? That means I'm in charge of strategy and guiding you, and you're in charge of physical labor. I've done my job. Isn't that enough?"

That did make sense.

No, wait! I can't let him sweet-talk me! It won't kill him to help me look for a cat.

"Kei, you can't just— Huh?"

He was gone. He sure is fast when he's running away. Did he really mean to leave me here all by myself?

"I'll show him! I'll find that thing if it kills me!" I grumbled.

"What thing?" someone suddenly said behind me.

I spun around in surprise to see my friend Misaki.

"Oh, hey, Misaki. What are you doing here?"

Her big brown eyes shone fiercely behind her glasses, which made her look kind of serious. "I wanted to ask you that. Weren't you just talking to yourself?"

"I'm looking for something."

"You are? I can help you. What are you trying to find?"

"A missing cat called…Scottie, or something." I showed her the flyer.

"I've seen that cat before. It's a Scottish fold."

So she knew about it, too? This must be one popular Scottie.

"I love cats, you know. But why are you looking for it? Do you know the owner?"

"It's hard to explain. Aren't you on your way somewhere?"

She was wearing a sky-blue skirt and a crisp, frilly white shirt. Anyone could see she was dressed up for something.

"I'm on my way home. My grandma's in the hospital."

"No way! Granny Yurie?"

I knew her. She lived by herself in our neighborhood, and

I'd been to her house a couple of times with Misaki. She was friendly and nice. And she always gave us sweets.

"She's sick?" I asked.

"You could say that," Misaki answered.

"What do you mean?"

You could say what?

"A month ago, robbers broke into her house."

"You're kidding!"

For a second, I thought of Phantom Thief Red, but Red would never do something like that.

"They took her jewelry box with everything in it. She got so depressed, she finally checked into the hospital yesterday."

"Was the jewelry worth a lot?"

"Yeah, some of it, but that's not what upset her. They took a ring that meant a lot to her."

Misaki's eyes teared up. Her grandma really must have cared about that ring if the shock of losing it had put her in the hospital.

"I guess she had a lot of memories associated with the ring. Isn't it awful that someone took it, Asuka?"

"Of course!"

I nodded enthusiastically. I couldn't let someone hurt Granny Yurie like that!

"I hate robbers. I wish they'd leave us alone," Misaki said, biting her lip.

"I agree! They should just…"

Suddenly, I broke off. An image of Dad and Uncle K flitted through my mind.

…Red—Dad and Uncle K—were thieves. Maybe they stole something in the past that meant a lot to someone. And now I was about to become a thief, too. Was it really the right thing to do?

Wait!

Red was the friend of the weak and the enemy of evil, just like Dad said.

Dad might have the world's worst fashion sense and be a super-tough coach, but he would never betray me. Never.

"What's wrong, Asuka?"

I looked up and realized Misaki's face was inches from mine.

"Wh-why are you asking?"

"You look more serious than usual. Did something happen?"

"Nothing at all!"

I couldn't tell Misaki about Phantom Thief Red, of course. Especially not right now.

"By the way, don't you think that cat over there looks like the one in the flyer…?"

"What? …Ahaaaa!"

A cat with folded ears and short fur was strolling right through the middle of the park. It was the spitting image of the photograph. No question about it—this was the target.

"Found ya, Scottie!"

I dashed toward the cat.

"Asuka, you can't just—!" Misaki called after me, but I didn't have time to talk.

The Scottie must have noticed me barreling toward it, because it ran off in a hurry.

Ugh, trust a cat. That thing was fast!

It was gaining distance by the second, racing toward the trees around the park. But then it skirted the fountain, probably because cats hate water.

"Fatal mistake, Scottie!" I shouted.

I planted one foot on the edge of the fountain and jumped. *Made it!* I was on the far side of the fountain, and the Scottie was at my feet. I reached down.

"Darn it!"

My hand was just a split-second too slow, and before I knew it, the cat was across the grass.

"Asuka, try to calm down!" Misaki said, panting as she ran up to me.

"I'm fine! The fight's not over yet!"

"Since when was this a fight?"

"Since now!" I raced after the Scottie. "Waaaaaaait!!"

My muscles were warmed up, and I was moving faster now.

"Almost got it…"

Just before I caught up, the Scottie reached a tree and shot up it, claws out. I swear it was smirking at me from the branches.

"Ha! You think you escaped me?" I sneered, examining the tree. It was fairly tall. Most kids wouldn't be able to climb it.

But...

...I noted the position of the branches and hollows. *Okay, I could grab here and put my foot there...* A route naturally formed in my mind.

"Um, Asuka, what are you planning to do?" Misaki asked, sounding worried.

"Catch the Scottie, obviously. Here I go!"

I grabbed a low branch and pulled myself up. I put my foot in a hollow and snagged the next branch.

"...You never did seem to care much about gravity," Misaki sighed.

Pfft, gravity. Who cares about that?

In under ten seconds, I was on the same branch as the cat.

"I'm not letting you get away, so just stay cal— Ah!"

The Scottie dived nimbly down to the ground. As I scrambled after it, Misaki called up to me.

"Asuka, seriously! Think of the poor kitty, getting chased everywhere." She was frowning at me, while the Scottie was growling, and its fur was standing on end. "Aww, baby, I bet you're scared," Misaki cooed.

"Be careful!"

"Don't worry, it's just a little scared. Right, kitty?"

She smiled at the Scottie, and it walked slowly toward her. When it got to her feet, it started rubbing its head on her leg. Misaki pet it a few times, then scooped it in her arms.

"No way! How did you do that...?"

"Come on, Asuka. If you chase it around like a wolf trying to eat it, of course it's going to run away."

A wolf? People keep calling me names lately.

"Anyway, come down from there," she called.

I jumped from the branch to the ground. On the way down, I did a full flip in midair. It was a little bit scary, but of course I made a perfect landing. I wouldn't let a Scottie outdo me.

"Hey, don't start showing off in front of cats!" Misaki scolded.

She knows me too well.

She didn't look at all surprised by my acrobatics. She's probably used to it because she's seen me do stuff like this since we were little, but she's so chill about it that it's never occurred to me until recently that I might be kinda weird.

"Now that we've got the Scottie, I better return it to the owner," I said, reaching out to take it from Misaki. It bared its teeth and growled.

"It hates you. I don't have anything better to do, so I'll come with you."

"Really? Thanks! You're the best, Misaki."

After dropping off the Scottie with its owner, I said good-bye to Misaki and went home.

Kei wasn't there, so he must have gone out. I found Dad in the kitchen efficiently washing and cutting the *oden* ingredients we'd bought for dinner.

"Dad, I found the Sco…I mean, the cat and returned it to its owner."

Dad looked over at me. "Oh yeah? That was fast… Hey, where's Kei?"

"He told me where he thought the cat would be, then took off. I really don't get that kid."

"Makes sense, if he's in charge of strategy and guidance. That's a valid way to do things."

"It is not! He's not helpful at all. It's unbelievable." I crossed my arms and puffed out my cheeks. "Anyway, are you going to give me an assignment now?"

I glared at him.

"Oh, right. I asked Keiichi to look into it for me. I'll have it ready by tomorrow."

"Yesss!"

I was finally getting my first job as Phantom Thief Red. Just thinking about it made my heart pound. What would

I be stealing? And who would I be stealing it from? Suddenly, I remembered what Misaki had told me about her Granny Yurie. A pang shot through my chest.

"…Um, Dad?"

"Yeah?" he said, his hands still flying.

"Why did you become Red? Was it because it was the family business?"

"Where'd that come from?" He stopped chopping.

"I just wanted to know." I stared at his still hands.

"…I guess because I couldn't accept it," he mumbled. His back looked much broader than usual.

"Couldn't accept what?"

"…A lot of things."

For once, he sounded serious. I was kind of surprised, but when I gave it a little thought, it made sense.

Phantom Thief Red is a hero, after all—a hero who steals from unacceptably bad people.

Maybe I was overthinking things.

What mattered now was my first assignment, coming the very next day.

5

Welcome to the World of Phantom Thieves!

"Okay, here we all are," Dad said to me and Kei.

It was the following day, and the three of us plus Uncle K were gathered in the living room. Uncle K had a laptop in front of him and was typing furiously.

"It's finally the first meeting of second-generation Phantom Thief Red!!" I said.

I was getting nervous!

"…Everyone knows that," Kei retorted smugly.

Ouch.

"Let's get started. Keiichi, it's all you." Dad nodded at Uncle K. Even now that we were living in the same apartment, I'd hardly heard a word from him. He stopped hammering away on the keyboard and looked up sharply.

Normally, he struck me as kinda drowsy, but now he was wide-awake.

What was going on?

"Welcome to the fantastic world of phantom thievery!!" he shouted.

What the heck?!

Kei looked as shocked as I was.

"Listen well; I have something to say first and foremost. Phantom thieves must be beautiful. It's not about just doing the work; it's about doing it with cleverness and pizzazz. It all depends on your skill as the strategist, Kei, and Asuka's physical prowess and natural instincts. Carrying on the Red tradition means carrying on the art of thiefdom that I have developed. Remember that."

Uh…yes, sir…

"Right then. Asuka, Kei, listen carefully."

Uncle K was…smirking? I'd never seen such a suspicious-looking smile.

Ugh!

I rubbed my eyes and stared at him again.

Yeah, he's definitely smirking...

Who is this guy, and what did he do with my quiet Uncle K?

Dad shrugged like he'd seen this a million times and glanced at me. Did that mean I should listen to Uncle K?

As I struggled to take this all in, Uncle K started reeling off information.

"So! The item we'd like you to steal is a diamond called the Green Sea. Incidentally, diamonds are the hardest substance in the natural world. The word *diamond* comes from the Greek *adámas*, meaning 'unconquerable.' Diamonds are the birthstone for April, symbolizing eternal bonds and purity. Only a limited number of countries produce diamonds, although they are abundant in Russia and parts of Africa. You may imagine all diamonds are colorless and transparent, but in fact, there are blue, pink, and green variations, which are very rare..."

"Keiichi, they don't need your vast knowledge of jewels right now. Just tell them about the assignment," Dad interrupted.

"Fully comprehending the target is the foundation of the art of thiefdom... Oh, never mind. Any questions so far, you two?" Uncle K asked, glancing from Kei to me.

Questions? He talked so fast that I didn't understand half of what he said! But I did know one thing.

"Diamonds are one of the most expensive gems, right?"

Even I knew that.

"Kei, did anything strike you?" Uncle K asked, like he was testing him.

"…I'm pretty sure a jewel called the Green Sea, currently valued at three billion yen, was stolen from Russia last month," he answered quietly, not taking Uncle K's bait.

"Th-three billion?! Kei, are you serious?!" I stammered.

How many zeros is that?

Okay, fine, I know how many, but I couldn't imagine that much money.

"It's three hundred thousand 10,000-yen bills. If you stacked them up, they would be almost a hundred feet tall and weigh over six hundred fifty pounds," Kei explained, looking at me.

Six hundred fifty pounds? That's how many times my weight…?

Maybe it was better not to imagine it.

Anyway, how did this kid know stuff like that? And why was he so calm right now?

"Now, would you mind setting aside your shock so I can continue?" Uncle K asked, his eyes flashing behind his glasses.

Honestly, what was up with him? I just stared back at him. He nodded anyway.

"Like Kei says, the Green Sea is probably worth around three billion yen. It might bring in more in an auction, but it would never go on the market, so there's no point speculating. But I want to make this clear. You are not targeting it because of the price."

"…Because we won't get to keep it anyway?" I asked, over-whelmed by his vehemence.

"Nope. There's another reason to steal it."

"Like what?"

I didn't get it.

"The man who currently has the diamond is named Shu-zou Sawamoto. He's a villain who traffics in stolen goods."

Translation…?

"He buys things that other people steal and sells them for a lot of money. He's like a shop for thieves."

"That's crazy! He's selling other people's things!"

Unbelievable. How could he get away with it?

"Of course, it's unacceptable. But this Sawamoto fellow doesn't leave many clues that could lead to his arrest. That's why Red's got to step in." Uncle K grinned. He really seemed to be enjoying himself today. "Normally, Sawamoto only handles small jewels, but this time, for whatever reason, he's trafficking the Green Sea diamond, which was stolen from a wealthy Russian. My guess is, he couldn't turn down a friend."

Bad guys have friends? That was a surprise.

"Asuka, what do you think will happen if the Green Sea is stolen from Sawamoto?"

"I guess…he'll be upset. Especially since he's looking after it for someone else."

"Correct. People in the underworld would stop trusting him. And unlike the anonymous little jewels he's handled up till now, the Green Sea has been all over the news, so once the police find out he had it, they'll pounce."

"Oh…"

I kind of understood and kind of didn't. Basically, if Red stole the Green Sea, the bad guy Sawamoto would be taught a lesson.

"The point is, you want us to steal the diamond, right?" Kei said.

"That's right. If you steal it, we'll take care of the rest. Kei, I want you to come up with a strategy for stealing the Green Sea from the building where Sawamoto is keeping it, and I want you to serve as Asuka's strategist on the day of the theft."

"Huh. Okay," Kei said, as unenthusiastic as ever.

"Good. I'll be expecting some marvelous guidance from you."

"Okay."

"Hey, wait a second, Kei!" I said. "Are you sure we don't want to think this through a little more? Don't you think that building has, like, tons of security?"

"Probably."

"'Probably'…?"

I was the one who had to sneak in there. And I was really worried…

"I'll figure it out. No problem," Kei declared. Did his eyes just sparkle a little?

"I think Kei can handle this," Dad said, looking at the other two.

"What do you mean?" I asked.

"When your Uncle K comes up with strategies for Phantom Thief Red, his personality changes, like it did today. When that switch is on, he's as reliable as they come."

He was saying Kei was going to be the same? I wasn't sure I liked that idea...

"*I* change? You should see yourself when you're Red," Uncle K muttered to Dad.

That was weird...

He sounded like the quiet uncle I knew again.

"Me? I do everything by the book, thank you," Dad answered.

Uh, what part of you is by the book?

Sometimes, Dad does crazy stuff. Once, when I was little, he interrupted a superhero show at an amusement park by shouting, *"No, no, you're all over the place!"* and started teaching the heroes how to fight. Obviously, the people running the amusement park chewed him out afterward.

"You're your father's daughter, Asuka, so you might do something crazy yourself," Uncle K said.

"Th-that's not true! I'm extremely normal!"

"...Normal elementary schoolers can't scale twenty-story buildings," Kei pointed out.

"Hey! I don't need your commentary!" I snapped.

"Ha-ha. Glad to see they're getting along," Dad said. He and Uncle K were both smiling.

What, exactly, gave them the idea we were getting along?

Also, weren't they awfully easygoing considering we were about to steal a diamond worth three billion yen?

"Come on, stop sulking, Asuka," Dad said. "I got this for you."

He pulled a paper bag from under his chair and held it out to me.

"What is it?" I asked, taking the bag.

"Open it and see," he said, waggling his eyebrows.

I took out the contents of the bag. "Is this…?"

It was a black bodysuit with a bright-red skirt.

"It's your Phantom Thief Red costume. You'll need that, right?"

Wow. My heart was suddenly racing.

"Doesn't Kei get one?" I asked.

"He won't be on-site. We'll get him one if he needs it, but for now, I don't think he does."

That made sense. Also, I wasn't sure I wanted to be twinsies with Kei.

"You sure look happy," Kei said. He was giving me that "You're weird" look again.

"So what if I am? I bet you're jealous," I snapped.

"In your dreams."

He shook his head. He's so rude.

But we were about to debut as Phantom Thief Red.

I was getting nervous!

6

Another Reason

"Thanks for coming," Misaki said as we walked along.

"You don't have to thank me. I'm worried about Granny Yurie, too."

We were headed toward the hospital in a neighborhood near ours where Granny Yurie was staying. I'd been worried about her ever since Misaki told me what happened, so I'd asked Misaki if I could visit her in the hospital. Kei was busy coming up with a plan for Phantom Thief Red. He said he needed to concentrate and basically kicked me out of our room.

…Which used to be my room.

"Here it is," Misaki said, stopping in front of a white building.

Wow, this was a big hospital. I suddenly wondered if that meant Granny Yurie was really sick.

We went inside, and Misaki led me to her room. There were six nameplates next to the door, and one of them said, Yurie Himuro.

"Granny's pretty depressed, but don't let it get to you."

"I'll be fine."

I came to cheer her up, after all. I knew she was depressed.

Misaki opened the door to head in, and I followed her. Granny Yurie was lying on a bed next to the window. Her face was pale, and she looked a little thinner than the last time I saw her.

"Hi, Granny, good to see you."

"Oh, you're here, too, Asuka? You came just to see me?"

"Yes. Misaki told me you were in the hospital, and I was worried about you. Here's a little present."

I placed a paper bag with cherry-blossom mochi inside on her bedside table. Granny Yurie loves them, and I've had them lots of times at her house. The scent of the flowers is so delicate. They're really good.

"How thoughtful of you. I'm fine, though. I had a little shock and didn't feel like eating, and that made me dizzy… Wasn't that silly of me?"

She sounded the same as always. I was relieved; she was doing better than I'd expected.

"I don't think it's silly!" I said. "Misaki told me a ring that meant a lot to you was stolen."

"Yes, that's right… I don't care about the other things they took; I just wish they'd give that ring back… Of course, I know that won't happen. They haven't even caught the thief."

"Why was the ring so important to you? You seem very attached to it."

"I was wondering the same thing," Misaki said, nodding.

"I do suppose I ought to tell you, since I've made you so worried. But it's a dull story about things that happened long ago. Are you sure you want to hear it?"

"Definitely. Of course, you don't have to say anything if you don't want to, though," I said.

"It's not like you to be so considerate, Asuka! I don't mind. Anyhow, I've been wanting to share it with somebody. It's a long story, so why don't you have some sweets while I tell you about it?"

Granny Yurie handed Misaki and me each one of the chewy cherry-blossom-flavored mochi cakes.

"But I brought these for you," I said.

"I don't mind sharing. Seeing you two eat makes me feel better," she said.

Misaki and I exchanged glances.

"If you say so," I said, biting into my mochi. The sweet bean paste and soft cherry blossom scent came together in my mouth as a delicious flavor. "Mmm, these are as good as I remember!"

"Asuka, did you buy these for Granny because you wanted one yourself?" Misaki asked, giving me a pointed stare. I shook my head. I did want to eat one before I gave them to her, but I resisted.

"Stop quarreling, girls," Granny Yurie said, gazing out the window. Slowly, like she was pulling up the memories, she began to tell her story.

Back then, Granny was still in her second year of high

school. The rainy season had ended, and summer was finally kicking in.

"It was hot that day. To make matters worse, it was my turn to clean the classroom after school, and I was taking the garbage out with a friend. The pail was heavy that day, and I was staggering a bit as I walked. I'm a short person, as you know, and my friend joked that she couldn't tell if I was carrying the garbage pail or it was carrying me."

Misaki's short, too. Must be in the Himuro family genes.

"But I managed to get it all the way to the stairs. When I started going down, I couldn't see in front of me, and I missed a step."

"Oh no!" I exclaimed. "Were you all right?"

"Well, you see, a boy caught me at the bottom. He was in my class. Seemed like everyone had a crush him; he did judo and was very muscular."

"How romantic!"

This story was unfolding like a TV show. I was a little envious. But if I said that, they'd probably say I would be the one doing the catching, so I kept that thought to myself.

"After that, we started talking and became close," Granny Yurie went on.

"Was he your boyfriend?" Misaki asked.

"Good heavens, no. It wasn't like that. More like a deep friendship. But at the end of second semester, he unexpectedly had to move."

"So you couldn't see him anymore?"

"I'm afraid so. The day before he moved, he asked me to go to a park near school with him."

"Then what happened?"

Misaki and I were both leaning toward the bed.

"He handed me a turquoise ring and said he had planned to give it to me when he asked me out."

"What's turquoise?" I asked. Was that an English word? I imagined a turkey.

"It's a kind of beautiful blue gem. It means 'Turkish stone.' It's the birthstone for December, which is when my birthday is. It turned out he'd secretly been working since summer break to save up for it. Turquoise isn't too expensive, so he was able to afford it."

"Wow! What a go-getter. So did you go out with him?"

Granny Yurie shook her head.

"Why not? Didn't he say he was planning to—? Oh."

Was planning… In other words, he decided not to.

"You see, when he started working, he didn't know he was going to move. But even after he knew, he kept work-ing and eventually bought the ring at a department store. He said he didn't make up his mind to give it to me until the last minute."

"If you liked each other that much, didn't you think about dating long-distance?" Misaki asked, looking unconvinced.

"Back then, it wasn't an option. Remember, cell phones

and email didn't exist. University entrance exams were coming up the next year, and I think we both were trying to be considerate of each other."

"Hmm…"

What a sad story. If only he hadn't moved, their love might have blossomed.

"That's why the ring means so much to me. It holds a lot of memories."

Granny Yurie's eyes were a little moist. I knew I couldn't fully understand how she felt, since I was only about to start junior high. But I could imagine how sad it must be to suddenly lose something really, really important.

It was hurting me, too. This was awful!

Just who was the jerk who stole her ring?!

If they were here right now, I'd knock their lights out!

…Wait a second.

If they stole her ring, they were probably planning to sell it, not wear it themselves. Didn't I just hear about someone in that business?

"Misaki, I've got to go home!"

"What? Why all of a sudden?"

She looked surprised.

"I have to do something. Granny Yurie, keep your spirits up. I know it's gonna get better for you!"

"Oh! All right…"

"I'll come again!" With that, I flew out of the hospital room.

"Asuka, wait!"

Ignoring Misaki, I hurried out of the hospital and started running home as fast as I could. After what we talked about the previous day, maybe Sawamoto was behind this. I had to talk to Kei.

Kei was in our room. He was sitting in front of his laptop with his back to me, wearing a checkered shirt and pressing his temples like he was deep in thought.

"Hey, Kei!" I shouted.

"…What?"

He glanced over his shoulder with his usual unfriendly expression.

"I need to talk to you."

"If I say no, you'll probably just ask me later, right?"

That rubbed me the wrong way. It was true, though, so I let it be. I sat on the bed and looked at him. His hair was even messier than usual. Had he been ruffling it up while he tried to figure stuff out?

"I want to tell you a little story," I said.

I talked to him about Granny Yurie. I'm bad at explaining things, and the timeline got all jumbled, but Kei just listened.

"…So that's the deal. What do you think?" I asked, staring at him.

I wasn't sure he understood. His expression hadn't changed, and I had no idea what he was thinking.

"…I think it's possible," he muttered.

"Really?"

I jumped up. Maybe we could get Granny Yurie's ring back!

"But it might be harder to find than the Green Sea," he added.

"Why? It's not worth a lot, so the thief probably isn't guarding it very carefully. It should be easy."

"You've got it backward."

"Huh?"

For a second, I caught a hint of annoyance on his face. *Sorry for being slow, I guess.*

"Let me ask you a question. If you saw that ring, would you recognize it?" he asked.

"Of course I wouldn't. I've never seen it."

"There must be a million rings that look like that one. Even if Sawamoto does have it, he probably isn't keeping it by itself like the Green Sea. It'll be hard to pick a specific one out from all the others just based on a description."

Oh. Good point.

"Then how about we bring Granny Yurie the rings one by one to look at?"

"Nope. What do we say if someone asks where we got them all?"

"Oh, right…"

What should we do? Sawamoto might have the lost ring, and I was planning to break into his building anyway. Was I supposed to pretend I didn't see anything and just go home?

That would be awful.

The Phantom Thief Red I knew would never do that!

Kei, thinking the conversation was over, had turned back to his laptop. Wasn't he bothered by what I told him? What a jerk! Could I really partner up with a guy like that?

7

A Surprising Side to Kei

The next day, Kei and I decided to go to Sawamoto's building to check things out.

"It's in the next town over, right?" I asked him as we walked.

"It's thirty stories high. That's pretty big for around here," he answered.

I hadn't forgotten how cold he'd acted the day before, but I knew there was no point in being mad at him.

He seemed like the type who thought arguing was stupid. He probably wouldn't even blink if I got mad at him.

"So what exactly does casing a building involve?" I asked.

"Looking at it."

I knew that! I was asking *what* we should look at.

"My dad said it's important to check out the real thing or the actual place where we'll be working," he said.

"Is that part of his 'art of thiefdom'?"

"Yeah. I've looked at photos, and I found a blueprint of the structure, so I told him I thought I didn't need to actually go there. He got all bossy and said, 'There are certain things you can't know without seeing the real thing. You still don't understand what phantom thievery is all about.'"

He chewed his lip like that bothered him.

The art of thiefdom aside, I mostly got Uncle K's point.

I mean, I was nervous. What if Kei was expecting me to play it by ear when I snuck into the building?

"Nice job nabbing the blueprint," I said. "Those aren't easy to get, right?"

"They are, if you go online and hack the computers of the company that built the building."

Hacking? I had a bad feeling about that.

"…Um, Kei? That's illegal, isn't it?"

"If the police found out, they'd arrest me."

"Are you kidding?! What are you doing?!"

"Did you forget we're thieves?"

Oh, right.

No matter how evil our nemesis was, I was still going to break into a building and steal a diamond that didn't belong to me.

Still, Kei was able to sneak into some company's computer system? He was so antisocial, not to mention younger than me—how was he so good at this stuff?

"Wait, where are you going, Kei? The station is right there," I said as he strode past the entrance. It was two whole stops between here and the next town.

"I know that. If you want to take the train, go right ahead."

"Why don't we both take the train?"

Was he mad at me? He had no reason to be.

"…I can't." He grimaced.

"Can't what?"

"Go on cars and trains and stuff."

"You get carsick?"

He nodded. I hadn't heard of many people getting motion sickness on a train, but they must exist.

"So you're planning to walk there? We should have taken bikes," I said.

"I can't do that, either."

"What? Oh. You didn't bring one when you moved in, did you? If you asked, we could have borrowed one from someone."

"That's not the problem."

Then what was? For once, he was talking in circles.

"…I get sick."

"Yeah, you just told me you can't ride trains, right?"

"No."

Wait, then that means… "You get sick riding a *bike*?"

"Sorry. That's why I said you could take the train."

He kept walking grumpily.

"Hey, wait! I'm coming with you."

I caught up with him, and we traveled parallel to the tracks. All the while, trains were passing us. We could have gotten there so fast if we were on one of them!

"If you want to take the train, why don't you turn around and get on?" he said.

"I didn't say I wanted to."

"You didn't have to."

Oof. I didn't have a comeback for that. Even Misaki and Dad said they could see my thoughts on my face.

"Well, you always have a poker face, so I can't tell what you're thinking…," I said, when a building across the street distracted me. "Hey, that sure looks easy to climb!"

Kei stared at me.

"Oh, I'm not planning to climb it right now. It's just a habit I have."

"A habit?"

"When I see a wall, I instantly think about where I can

put my hands and what route I'd take to climb it. Not that I'm always climbing things! Just occasionally."

"Most people don't occasionally climb high-rise buildings," he answered coldly.

It wasn't my fault! Dad taught me to be this way.

"By the way, I've been wondering, why didn't you say no to being Red?" I asked him.

"…That came out of the blue."

"I can ask, right? You're not the type who's interested in other people, so I figured you'd think being Red with me was a hassle."

"…Is that what you think of me?"

Obviously. What else could I think of him?

"It's simple," he went on. "Saying no would have been more trouble than it's worth. I'd rather just carry on the family tradition than try to talk Uncle Tsuba and my dad out of it."

"'Just' carry on the tradition…?"

That's not a very thorough way to make a decision. I stared at him. He looked back as if to say, "What can you do?"

"…Also, I thought it would be fun," he added.

"Being a phantom thief?"

Huh. We agreed on that. That was a surprise.

"But you're not worried? Like, what happens if we make a mistake or something?"

"Nope. Trying to do something special always involves a risk."

A risk…

He was always so logical about everything. I guess I shouldn't have asked.

After walking for about an hour, we got to the building. The two of us craned our necks at the towering thirty-story high-rise. It was as round as a pipe—and as silver as one, too. The surrounding buildings were all low cubes, with this one shooting up above them. There weren't any houses nearby, and judging from all the middle-aged men walking around in suits, it seemed to be a business district.

"Wow, it's so tall!" I said. I leaned way, way back, but I still couldn't see the roof.

"About four hundred twenty-five feet, I'd say," Kei said.

"I can tell you one thing right now: I can't climb this. It's really tall, and there's nowhere for me to put my feet. And there aren't any windows to sneak in through."

"I don't expect you to climb it."

He didn't? I'd assumed I'd have to climb the outside.

"But the entrance is guarded." I pointed at the two people standing outside the building. They were both tall and looked like they did some kind of martial arts. Would I be able to get in without them noticing me?

"I know that," Kei said.

"So you want me to knock them out and force my way in? That's more fighting than I expected."

"If you did that, don't you think you'd be reported to the security office? Never mind, just leave the thinking to me."

What the heck? Didn't he care about my worries? I was the one sneaking in. Did he get that?

Just then, someone behind me said, "Asuka, is that you?" I turned around.

"Misaki! What are you doing here?"

"That's what I should be asking you! I'm visiting my grandmother."

Oh, right, I guess Granny Yurie's hospital was near here. "Um…I had some stuff to do…"

No way could I tell her I was casing the joint for Phantom Thief Red. Misaki seemed confused. When she noticed Kei behind me, her mouth fell open in surprise.

"Sorry! Are you on a date?"

"Wh-what are you talking about?! That's just my cousin Kei."

"You don't have to get so upset," Misaki said, giggling.

She was the one making weird comments!

"Anyway, I didn't know you had a cousin," she said.

"Some stuff happened, and we didn't see each other much."

"Hmm. How old is he?"

"Same age as me."

She stared at him intently, long enough that I was getting antsy.

"…He looks kinda cool," she mumbled.

"Misaki, are you serious?"

What, exactly, about that unfriendly, gloomy kid was cool?

"That's a mean thing to say. But whatever. I have to get going," she said.

"Okay… Hey, wait. Would it be okay if we came with you to see Granny Yurie?"

"Sure… You mean you and your cousin?"

She looked at him. He must have heard us, but he was staring at the road with disinterest.

"Yeah. You'd never guess it, but he's really smart. I wanted him to hear the story about the ring."

"Okay, but don't you need to ask him if he wants to come?"

"It's fine. I don't need to ask. I'm dragging him with me."

"I suddenly feel sorry for your cousin."

What, I'm the bad guy now? Well, I suppose it wouldn't hurt to ask.

"Kei, I'm going to visit Misaki's grandmother in the hospital. You want to come, right?"

"…Yeah, sure," he said after a questionable silence.

"Wow, you didn't fight me at all. I was sure you'd complain," I said.

"I know when resistance is futile," he answered, shrugging very slightly.

8

Uh-Oh, We Got in a Fight.

The hospital room was just the same as the last time we visited.

"I'm sorry I ran out so suddenly last time, Granny Yurie," I said as soon as I saw her.

"Oh, don't worry about that. You had something to do, didn't you?"

"Um, yes. Something like that...," I said vaguely. I couldn't very well say I realized where her ring was.

"Thanks to all the lovely people here, I'll be able to go home tomorrow," she said.

"You will?! That's great! ...That reminds me, I wanted to ask you about the ring. Do you mind?"

"Not at all, but...is there anything we haven't already talked about?"

"Yes, a few things. Also, I brought my cousin today. Sorry for not introducing him sooner." I stepped aside so Granny Yurie could see Kei more easily.

"Pleased to meet you, dear. I'm Misaki's grandmother, Yurie."

"…I'm Kei Kouzuki," he said without smiling, then bobbed his head.

I swear, this kid! As antisocial as always.

"I'm sorry, my cousin gets shy sometimes," I said.

"Don't you worry. That's how boys are. Now, what was it you wanted to ask me?"

"Well, do you remember the design of the turquoise ring that was stolen?"

"The design? Let me think. It wasn't anything special, just a simple ring. Why?"

"Uh, um, I was just wondering…in case I see it somewhere."

Even I knew that was a bad excuse.

"Hmm. Our initials aren't engraved on it. We were both too shy for anything like that. The decorations were quite ordinary, and I don't think there was anything to set it apart."

"Oh…"

I'd been hoping it had some kind of mark to help us pick it out from other rings. Welp. I was out of ideas.

"Hey, Kei, you don't want to ask Granny Yurie anything?"

"…I wouldn't say that."

Aha. So bringing him was a good plan after all. He might have some ideas.

"Granny Yurie, would you mind answering Kei's questions?" I asked.

"Not at all. What would you like to know?" she asked, looking at him.

"I only have one question. Why do you care so much about an accessory? I don't get it. It's just a precious stone, right? Couldn't you buy a new one?"

"Well, I…," Granny Yurie began, then stopped.

"Kei, why are you being so rude?!" I shouted, grabbing his shoulder.

"You were the one who told me to ask a question."

I did, but how insensitive can you get?

"Asuka, we're in the hospital; can you be a little quieter…?" Misaki whispered in a panic.

I pressed my lips together, while Kei just stood there like nothing had happened. That made me want to go off on him all over again.

"Hey, here's a question for *you*, Kei," I hissed. "Are you sure you have a soul?"

It was just the same six years ago, at our mothers' funeral…

It was raining the whole day, starting in the morning. It was the day of my mother's and Kei's mother's funeral. We were seven years old. Lots of people came to light incense at the temple.

"I'm sorry for your loss."

"Keep your chin up."

"They were so young…"

Everyone was crying. Dad greeted the attendees, but his eyes were red, and Uncle K was staring at the floor and wiping tears away.

But I think I cried more than anyone else. I didn't understand like I do now what it meant for my mom to die, but I understood that I would never see her again.

In my mind, I heard my mom's gentle voice, and I felt like I could still feel her cool palm against my cheek.

I kept crying and wailing and wouldn't let go of the coffin. I missed her so much.

Dad didn't try to pull me off. He just stood quietly by my side.

Once I'd worn myself out, Dad took my hand and led me toward the line of people. Just then, my eyes met Kei's. He was sitting down and glaring at me, like he was angry. But he wasn't crying, and his eyes weren't red or anything. Why was he making that face? Wasn't he sad? I wanted to ask him, but he looked away, like he didn't want to talk. After that, he always acted standoffish and uninterested in me. That was when we stopped talking much.

"…You didn't cry at our moms' funeral, either, did you?" I said before I could stop myself.

"What do our moms have to do with this?" he asked stiffly.

"The point is, you're like a rock!! You should think about other people's feelings! Think about how Granny Yurie must feel!!"

"I did."

"You're lying! You've always been like this. I never know

what's going on with you! Were you even sad when your mom died?"

What did the look in his eyes that day mean?

"...Asuka, don't say that," Misaki said, grabbing my shoulder.

I knew I was going too far. But my mouth had moved by itself. And you can't take words back once you've said them. I thought Kei would just stand there with a blank face as usual and ignore me. But a second later, his eyes were more furious than I'd ever seen them.

"What...what can a pathetic simpleton like you understand?!" he shouted, his whole body shaking. Then he ran out of the hospital room.

"Kei..."

I stared after him in a daze. I had no idea he could get that mad.

"What is all this shouting? That kind of behavior is unacceptable in a hospital!" a nurse said as she bustled into the room.

Of course, she was mad, and since Kei was gone, I was the only one left for her to yell at. Granny Yurie defended me, so I didn't get in that much trouble, but I still felt terrible afterward.

Why did I have to go and say something like that to Kei...?

9

Make Up? You've Gotta Be Kidding.

I trudged along on my way home from the hospital.

After the nurse left, Granny Yurie gave me some advice. *"If you think you did something wrong, you should apologize right away. As they say, there's no time like the present."*

"She's right. I should apologize...," I muttered to myself.

I knew I was in the wrong. But I still thought what Kei said was awful.

"I didn't know he could even make that expression..."

I thought his poker face was permanent, but he had emotions after all. Of course he did—but I'd forgotten that. I told him to think about other people's feelings, but I didn't think about his. I was such an idiot.

I got to our apartment complex, climbed the stairs, and opened the door. Dad and Uncle K seemed to be out. I peeked into our room, and Kei was on his computer. I couldn't see his face, but from what I could tell, he was back to the Kei I knew.

"...Hi," I said to his back.

He didn't answer. I knew I should say, "Sorry about earlier. I went too far," but the words stuck in my throat. This was a first. I can always talk without even thinking.

"...The certificate of authenticity," Kei suddenly mumbled, his back still to me.

"Huh? The certificate of what?"

What was he talking about?

"If the ring was worth anything, there should be a certificate of authenticity proving its value. That would have a photo of the ring."

"Oh..."

If we had that, we'd know what the ring looked like!

Kei had been thinking about the problem after all. And I...

"I'm really sorry, Kei!" I bowed my head vigorously.

After he didn't respond for a little while, I timidly lifted my head and looked at him.

"...I shouldn't have said what I said either," he muttered back to me. I let out the breath I was holding, relieved.

"Okay, I'm going to run over to Misaki's place!" I said, then flew out of our room.

I reached out to Misaki, and she got permission from Granny Yurie to look around her room. The very next day, Misaki and I were standing in front of her granny's house.

"Granny said she couldn't remember if there was a

certificate of authenticity or not," Misaki said as she opened the front door with the key she'd borrowed.

"Okay. But if we do find one, we'll know what the ring looks like. It's worth trying," I said.

"But even if we find the certificate, I highly doubt we'll find the ring."

Misaki seemed to think this was a pointless detour, and I couldn't exactly convince her otherwise. After all, I couldn't tell her about Phantom Thief Red. But if we had the certificate, then Kei and I—I mean Red—might be able to get her ring back.

"I haven't been here in forever," I said, looking around the house. The smell of woven tatami mats and wood hung in the air of the old wood-frame house.

"Should we start looking?" Misaki asked.

"Yeah. You open the drawers. When you give the okay, then I'll search them."

Even though we got permission, I still felt reluctant to check the drawers and chests of someone I wasn't even related to.

"Okay. Tee-hee, I feel like a robber." Misaki giggled.

My heart skipped a beat. I knew she was joking, but Misaki was sharp. I had to be careful about what I said.

We started searching the rooms. According to Granny Yurie, she kept documents in her Japanese-style room with tatami floors. Even that memory was vague, but it was all we had to go on.

"Did you find anything?" I asked.

"No. You?"

"Nothing. I did find some books and old magazines."

"A certificate of authenticity would usually be in a folder or something, right?"

"That's what Kei said. It should have a photograph of the ring on it."

I asked him about it before coming. As usual, he seemed antisocial and annoyed, but he still answered my questions.

"So you two made up?"

"Kinda."

"Just kinda? Didn't you apologize?" Misaki looked up at me.

"I apologized, but there wasn't much of a friendship to start with. We're not that close."

"You're not?" She looked surprised.

"No. We only really started talking recently."

I hadn't told her we were sharing a room. It wasn't like I had to hide it, but somehow, it felt hard to say.

"Hey, I think this is it," she said, pulling a green folder from a drawer and bringing it to me. Inside was a paper labeled *Gemstone Certificate of Authenticity* with the size, weight, and other information written below. At the top was a photo of a ring and the words *Natural Turquoise*.

"What do those English words say?" I asked.

She translated for me. She goes to special English conversation classes, so things like that are a snap for her.

"Then this really is it!" I said.

Now we could get the ring back!

And Granny Yurie wouldn't have to be sad anymore.

I borrowed the certificate of authenticity and headed home.

"I'm back!" I called.

"You went somewhere?" Dad asked from the living room, where he was reading the paper. I guess he didn't have to be at the restaurant till evening today.

"Just for a little while. Did Kei go out?"

"No, he's in your room. By the way, how's your first assignment going?"

"Good! Kei's doing a great job thinking for the both of us."

"You're leaning on him? That's good—the truth is, I lean on Keiichiro all the time," he said, laughing.

Then he was a fine one to talk. But I left him alone and went to my room. Kei was staring at his computer with more intensity than usual. He didn't even notice I was there. Feeling mischievous, I peeked over his shoulder at the screen.

DR. P. A.: You really saved the day on that paper about the theory of relativity the other day. Without your help, it would never have been published. But it made me wonder, are you against the theory?

KEI: Not at all. There are simply a few points that bother me.

PROF. Y. O.: I'd love to hear you expand on that. Would you come by for a chat next time you're at my university?

KEI: Of course. Your lecture last time on particle physics was most interesting. For instance, during the explanation of the absorption of electromagnetic waves, I liked your point about the importance of the law of conservation of angular momentum in determining whether a state will transition. That's outside my area of expertise, so it was very informative.

DR. P. A.: That reminds me, your thoughts on the Riemann hypothesis that you shared the last time you visited my lab were extremely interesting. What a stimulating evening of conversation that was. I think you'd make a good mathematician.

PROF. Y. O.: Out of the question. He wants to go into physics.

DR. P. A.: Oh, that's right. Sorry. Well, my time is up. I look forward to our next meeting, Kei.

DR. P. A. has left the room.

PROF. Y. O.: I've got to go, too. I hope you'll consider
                delivering a special lecture to my students
                soon. I'll email you about it.

          KEI: I'll look forward to that. It was great
                chatting.

PROF. Y. O. has left the room.

What just happened? I had no clue what they were talking
about. I was pretty sure it was Japanese, but...angular
momentum? The Riemann hypothesis? Was this some new
kind of fortune-telling?

"Asuka, what are you doing?" Kei asked, turning
around.

"Oh, Kei! You knew I was here?" I answered.

"Most people can tell if someone's standing behind them.
Did you see anything?" He glanced at the screen.

"No, I... It was an accident... I'm sorry!" I pressed my
hands together in apology.

"It's no big deal," he said.

"What were you doing?"

"Chatting. I was talking to scholars I know in the United
States and Germany. With the time differences, this is the
only time that works."

Scholars in the United States and Germany...?!

They definitely seemed like grown-ups. And Kei was
speaking to them like an equal.

Who the heck is this kid?!

"Anyway, good timing. I was just going to look for you," Kei said.

"What? Why?"

He almost never initiated conversations.

"I finalized the plan," he said.

"You did?!"

"I'd like to carry it out this Sunday night. Are you free then?"

"Of course!"

It was finally happening! My nerves were through the roof.

"I'll explain how to break in later. For now, I just wanted to tell you."

He'd been looking for me just to say that? He must be getting excited about this himself.

"Oh, by the way, I have some news, too. We found the certificate of authenticity!" I said.

"…Huh."

Not the reaction I was hoping for.

"Now we'll be able to look for Granny Yurie's ring. I need your help!"

"Nope."

"What?! Why?!"

Didn't he say if we had a photo of the ring, we could search for it?

"Phantom Thief Red's mission is to steal the Green Sea.

We're not going there to find a turquoise ring. We won't have time, and we can't risk it."

"But you're the one who told me about the certificate of authenticity!"

"I told you, but that's it. I can't make it part of the plan."

"That's so…"

I bit my lip. Kei was a cold fish after all. I guess Granny Yurie's story hadn't affected him.

"Fine! I don't need your help!" I snapped.

"If you go rogue on the day of the break-in, I can't guarantee your safety."

"!!"

I walked out of the room. Dad must have heard us, because he poked his head out of the kitchen.

"You two fighting?" he asked.

"No!!" I yelled.

It wasn't even a fight. I mean, Kei completely kept his cool! I was the only one freaking out like an idiot.

"I swear, you two. You better make up quick. Also, if you're free, could you clean out the bathtub?"

Did I look free to him? Kei wasn't doing anything, either!

"Tell Kei to do it! Ugh, why are you so weird, Dad?!"

After I vented my anger on him, I bolted out of the house.

10

Kei's Past

I was trudging through the shopping arcade. It was evening, and not many people were out.

"Is that you, Asuka? Is something wrong?" the plump produce lady called. She was carrying some cardboard, a brisk sense of purpose in her step.

"…Not really," I mumbled.

"You certainly look down in the dumps. Want to take some of my veggies home?" she asked, smiling as she held out a daikon radish.

"That sad little daikon won't cheer you up, Asuka!" a voice called from across the way. "How about some rockfish for dinner tonight? It's full of vitamin C, great for your skin. I recommend it highly!" The fish guy brought some of his stock over to me.

"What are you talking about?" the produce lady answered, glaring at him. "Asuka has perfect skin! She doesn't need any help from fish! My daikon is fresh and full of vitamins."

I burst out laughing.

"Thank you both. I'll buy something later," I said.

"Are you sure? I hope you know that if something's on your mind, you can always talk to me," the produce lady said.

"Or me. I'm ready and waiting with advice," the fish guy added.

They both grinned. Geez. Now I was going to cry.

"Th-thank you. I've got to go now."

I hurried off, tilting my head back slightly so I wouldn't tear up and worry them more. Still, thanks to them, my

heart felt a little lighter. When I got to the end of the shopping arcade, the station came into view. A train must have just arrived, because people were streaming from the ticket gates toward the shopping arcade.

"Uncle K?" I blurted out.

He was in the crowd. Uncharacteristically, he was dressed in a suit. I remembered he'd said he had some work to do today before leaving the house. He's a computer programmer, but he's at home a lot. He walked up to me.

"…Hello, Asuka. Shopping?" he asked in a peaceful voice. That day, he wasn't Phantom Thief Red—he was regular old Uncle K.

Uncle K is lanky and about four inches taller than me. He wears glasses and has longish hair, but that day, it was neatly combed.

"Not exactly…," I said. I was having a hard time saying I'd bolted from my room.

"Oh. Want to go for a walk?" he asked.

"A walk?"

He started striding in the opposite direction from the shopping arcade. That's where the river is. I wasn't sure what to do, but following him felt like my only choice. When he got to the riverbank, he sat down casually on the grass. I was clearly more worried about his suit than he was.

"…Did you get in a fight with Kei?" he asked as soon as I took a seat next to him.

Was it that obvious?

"Guess so… I know what he's like. It must be hard for you."

"I feel bad saying this, but he's got a horrible personality."

"You don't beat around the bush."

He smiled. Kei and Uncle K are similar, but in this way, they're completely different. Uncle K is quiet and blank-faced like Kei, but he's calmer. Or maybe *warmer* is a better way to put it.

"He got his unsociable side from me," he said.

"But you and Kei are different," I said.

"You think so? You don't miss much."

No one's ever told me that before. I mean, I've been told I don't miss dessert much, but…

"I'm not trying to defend him because he's my son, but he can't help being like that." Uncle K squinted sadly.

"Did something happen?" I asked. Something that wrecked his personality?

"…Maybe I'm making excuses, but I want to you to know this, because you'll be his partner."

I nodded silently. I sensed this was important.

"Ever since Kei was in preschool, he's had a very high intelligence quotient."

"His what?"

"…IQ. It's short for *intelligence quotient*."

That just made me more confused. When Uncle K threw out words like that, I could tell they were father and son.

"It's a measure of how smart you are. I think Kei's IQ was close to two hundred in preschool."

"Is that high?"

"…Most people have an IQ of around one hundred."

"So Kei's as smart as two people?!"

If that was true, his braininess made sense. I was super jealous, considering how tests always gave me a headache…

"But there's a downside, too. He struggles a lot."

"How, if he's that smart?"

That sounded like a contradiction. I thought everything was easy for smart people.

"…I guess it's hard for you to imagine. Let me give you an example. When Kei was in preschool, instead of puzzles, he did math problems for kids about to graduate high school."

"High school math?!"

"I heard he used branches to write equations with pi and gamma in the preschool sandbox."

Whoa. He sounded like a strange little kid.

"He asked the teachers hard questions, so they stayed away from him, and the kids bullied him and called him names…"

"Why?!"

He was just smart! What was wrong with that?!

Sometimes, he had an attitude, but this was different. I hate bullies as much as I hate squash.

Uncle K smiled kindly at me.

"If he'd had someone like you around, things might have

been different...but back then, the only people who really talked to him were me and his mom, Kyoko."

I couldn't imagine what that was like.

"Not long after that...Kyoko passed away, as you know."

Yes...she died with my mom.

"It came as a shock to me, too," he went on. "I left Kei to his own devices for a while. When I think back on it, I can't remember him crying once after he learned she'd died."

That's what I said to him at the hospital. So he'd never cried in front of his dad, either...

"I think he wanted to. But I kept my distance. I was too broken up myself to care for him emotionally. I was a bad father..."

I thought back to that time. I think I spent it with Dad, just crying and crying and crying some more. When I was all wrung out like a sponge, Dad had said, *"Right! Now, let's climb Mount Fuji!"*

I had no idea why he chose Mount Fuji, but I did know that it was the only thing that was anywhere near as big as my sadness.

The next day, we really did climb Mount Fuji. When we got home, totally exhausted, Mom wasn't there. I cried again, but my heart was still a little lighter. If it weren't for Dad, I might not be back on my feet even now.

"Tsubasa's amazing in that sense. He's done a good job raising you...although he did teach you some weird skills," Uncle K said.

Um, yeah. I feel like after Mom died, the training got a little out of control.

"Anyway, by the time I realized what was happening, Kei had withdrawn even further into his shell. Meanwhile, his mental ability was advancing just fine. These days, he coauthors physics papers with university professors on topics like the theory of relativity."

That's what he'd been chatting about earlier online.

Hmm. Given everything Uncle K just told me, maybe Kei couldn't help being the way he was.

"To tell the truth, Tsubasa was optimistic, but I didn't think you and Kei could make it work. I'm surprised you've done as well as you have."

"But look at us now…"

"…I thought you'd blow up at him within an hour."

Uncle K, I can't tell if you're joking or you really thought that.

"Just kidding. You should do what you believe is right, Asuka. Kei will understand in time."

Would he? Knowing Kei, would he ever see my point of view? I wasn't sure.

Uncle K gazed at the river, tinted red by the setting sun. A little boy was laughing as his dog pulled him down the riverbank. When Uncle K turned back to me, his eyes were calm and kind.

"…Kei doesn't trust other people. Most of what he wants to do, he can do on his own, and the people around him have mainly been attracted by his brain, not by Kei himself.

But you speak up when you're unhappy, and you let your emotions show in your face. I think that will be reassuring for him. I have confidence it will work out."

Was that a compliment?

Questionable.

"Let's go home. I'm tired from talking so much. Oh, and Tsubasa asked me to pick up some things for dinner," Uncle K said, standing up.

"What did Dad ask you to buy?"

"'Whatever looks good,' he said. But how do I know what looks good? I don't have a clue about cooking!"

Aha! Perfect!

I brushed the grass off my butt. "You're in luck, Uncle K. I know where we can get some good deals on produce and fish."

11

Second-Generation Red ☆, Up and Running

My heart was pounding. Today, Kei and I would attempt our first theft as the second generation of Phantom Thief Red. I was changing in our room. Obviously, I made Kei leave first.

It was dark outside. I glanced at the wall clock. Just after one in the morning. Thanks to Kei, who had suggested I take a two-hour nap in the afternoon, I wasn't very sleepy.

We planned to start the mission at two. The reason it had to be so late was because the building was less heavily guarded at night, and no one else would be there. Neither of us wanted to pull innocent bystanders into this.

I picked up the black bodysuit that was Red's costume and put my arms through the sleeves. I thought I'd have trouble getting it on, but it was easy. The fit was snug, so it wasn't too hard to move in. Surprisingly, Uncle K said he made it himself!

I put on the red bangle-style wristbands and belt that Uncle K and Kei made.

"This is kind of cute!" I said to myself, spinning around in front of the mirror. The red skirt fluttered up.

"Hey, can I come in yet?" Dad asked from outside the room.

"Yeah," I said, opening the door.

"Wow, that looks great on you!" he exclaimed.

"You look very nice, Asuka," Uncle K said.

I was so excited that I twirled around twice, then one more time for good measure.

"...You took way too long to change," Kei said, slipping past without even glancing at me before he sat down at his desk. Ugh. Such a jerk, as always.

"You'd better put on a disguise, Asuka. Were you planning to go to the building like that?" Dad asked, setting his hand gently on my shoulder.

Oh, right. I was so happy about my costume, I hadn't thought of that. But I'd never worn a disguise before.

"Just put your normal clothes on over the costume. No one will guess you're Red," he suggested.

He had a point. I do look like a normal twelve-year-old girl.

"All right, kids. Listen up," Dad said, suddenly serious.

I straightened my back. Kei turned toward us and got to his feet.

"Keiichiro and I won't be involved after this. From now on, it's up to you two to do Phantom Thief Red's work."

"I understand," I said, nodding. I glanced at Kei. He was nodding solemnly, too.

"This is the birth of the second generation of Phantom Thief Red," Dad said.

"I'll be wishing you all the best," Uncle K said, winking at me and then raising his eyebrows.

In other words, "Get along with your cousin." At least, that's how I took it.

We'd be fine. As usual, Kei was acting like we'd never argued, and I was keeping my focus on the Green Sea. I hadn't given up on finding Granny Yurie's ring, but right now, I had to concentrate on carrying out Red's first assignment with Kei.

Keep it inside!

That was the path I'd chosen.

Lit up by streetlights in the dead of the night, the building looked different, and bigger, than it had in daytime. Most of the lights in the windows were out. Almost no one was on the street. Trains weren't running at this time, and everyone had probably gone home.

I slipped down a narrow alley to avoid being seen and took off my disguise…er, my street clothes. I wrapped the red scarf that Kei had handed me before we left home around my neck and mouth.

"It's made from special elastic fabric. It might come in handy, so maybe you should take it," he'd said, shoving the package toward me with his usual distant expression.

Come to think of it, this might have been the first present a boy ever gave me. But it was from Kei. Honestly, who acts like that when they give a girl a present? *Sigh.* Why couldn't my life be like Granny Yurie's?

"Asuka, can you hear me? It's almost time." Kei's voice came through the special transmitters in my ears.

"I can hear you," I answered.

He was on the roof of an abandoned building with a view

of this one. I could just see him with his computer open and ready for action. He was going to guide me to the Green Sea from there. I pulled down the sports sunglasses on my head. Kei had fitted them out with a camera to send him video in real time. They also had infrared capability that made everything look bright even in the dark. He'd made them along with the transmitters. Right now, he should be seeing the same thing that I was seeing, only on his computer screen.

"Looks like there's three guards?" he said uncertainly.

"Yeah."

"Then we'll stick with the plan."

"Okay…," I said softly. That wasn't like me. The building in front of me was big, and of course, this was my first experience as a thief. I might be a supergirl, but I was still kinda scared.

"…Asuka? Are you nervous?" Kei asked.

"I'm f-fine."

My voice cracked, and I looked at my hands. They were shaking. I squeezed them into fists.

"Relax. Just follow my master plan, and you'll be just fine."

…Huh?

Wait a second! Who was that?!

"Relax"? "My master plan"?

Who was I talking to?

"What's wrong?" he asked.

"…Uh, this is Kei, right?"

"What are you talking about?"

No, I'm the one who's confused!

But that was definitely Kei's voice.

Oh, wait... Was he like Uncle K? Like, his personality changed when he was Red?

"Asuka. Are you sure you're all right?"

Oh well. He was easier to work with like this than as his usual impossible-to-figure-out self.

"I'm fine. I'm counting on you, partner."

"You can leave everything to me."

"Uh, okay..."

His voice was strong, decisive, and very masculine. In fact, he sounded so confident, I caught myself nodding along. I didn't feel like I was talking to my cousin at all. He was like a totally different guy. I was surprised, but I could feel my shoulders relaxing a little bit, too.

"Okay, I'm going in," I said.

I took a breath, psyched myself up, and started running toward the building. Normally, the guards might have noticed me, but I know a way of running that doesn't make a sound.

When I was about five yards from the entrance, I slowed down slightly and pulled a bright-red capsule from my belt. I squeezed the inch-diameter ball in my hand and flicked it with my thumb.

Pop, pop, pop!

There was a bursting sound near the guards' heads. A

second later, their big forms squatted unsteadily, then top-
pled to the ground.

Kei had filled the capsule with sleep-inducing gas. It sure
worked fast.

Incidentally, Dad was the one who taught me how to run
silently and how to do the thumb-flick. I used to think everyone could do that stuff, but apparently not. According to
Kei, there are probably only a handful of people in the world
who can do that thumb-flick, which we called a "finger
bomb." It's hard for me to wrap my head around that. To
me, it's just a useful trick for turning off the TV when I can't
find the remote control.

"Looks like that went well," Kei said over the transmitter.

"All three guards are down for the count," I answered.

"Good. Got their clothes and IDs?"

"Searching now… Sorry, miss," I said, pawing through
the coat of one of the conked-out guards. "Aha! Got it!"

The ID card was in her inner pocket. Apparently, it worked
like a key to the doors. I'd never used one before. I mean, if
I have a bobby pin, I can open a door in ten seconds flat.

"We're good on locks, then. You got her jacket and hat?" Kei
asked.

Geez, trust me a little. I told you I've got it.

I took the jacket and hat from the smallest guard and put
them on. I looked a little silly as a guard from the waist up.

"Are you sure this is okay?" I asked.

I couldn't help feeling nervous.

"Absolutely. You don't need to fool anyone."

His words brimmed with confidence. I wasn't used to that, but it was oddly reassuring. I nodded and swiped the ID card through the reader next to the door, and it clicked right open. Huh, that was easy.

"Sending the interior route now," Kei said.

A map of the building appeared on the screen of my sunglasses. These things really were convenient. A red line was drawn on the map. This was my route, designed to avoid security cameras.

"I'm going in," I said.

"Go for it, Asuka."

I knew this would happen.

I was getting nervous.

I took a step into the darkness.

12

Kei, Transformed?!

As soon as I got into the building, I made a dash for the shadows. Plastering myself to the wall, I squatted down. The security cameras in the entrance were unavoidable. That's why Kei had told me to sprint through as fast as I could.

I wasn't sure it would work, but he said it was the safest way. According to him, if I ran at top speed, the image on the camera would look like a passing shadow. Of course, if someone watched closely afterward, they would know it was a person, but by then, I'd be out of the building.

"Everything okay?" Kei asked.

"Yup. No one's here, and I don't see anyone coming."

"Good. Follow the route to Elevator C-2."

"Got it."

Since the initial break-in went so well, I felt a little less tense. Glancing around and sticking to the route, I walked forward. The building was pitch-black, but thanks to my infrared sunglasses, I could see as clear as day, except for the color.

The entryway was big and opened overhead to the second

floor. There were large paintings on the walls and vases of flowers in the hallway. But what really drew my attention was a bronze statue of a man I didn't recognize. He was standing in a weird pose with his finger pointing upward. The statue was about fifteen feet tall, and it looked really heavy.

"*That's Sawamoto,*" Kei said.

"He put up a bronze statue of himself? How tacky can you get?!"

I stared at the statue. I was gonna take back the Green Sea and Granny Yurie's ring from this guy, no matter what it took!

"*Asuka, forget about that ridiculous statue and get going,*" Kei prodded.

"I am," I snapped.

Slipping past the statue, I moved from the entryway into the hallway. It was lined with doors, but I didn't notice any sign of life behind them. Soon, the elevators came into view.

"I'm at the elevators," I told Kei, pulling myself together.

"*Good. Proceed according to plan,*" he answered.

"Leave it to me."

This was the first hurdle. There were security cameras all through the building and no way to avoid being filmed as I got on the elevator. If that was the only problem, I could have dashed on like I did at the entrance. But I had to press the button. I wanted to avoid standing still long enough to push it. Time for another finger bomb.

I stationed myself about fifteen feet from the elevator, out of view of the camera.

"Let's see… Here it is."

I took a small rubber ball from my belt.

"Don't miss. The whole plan is riding on this," Kei said sharply. I had never heard him like this.

"I know that," I said.

I sighed. He cared more about his plans than he did about me. I didn't get mad, though, since I expected that.

I squeezed the rubber ball in my palm. My heart was pounding. Normally, this would be an easy shot for me, but I felt like my hand was about to start shaking.

"Go get 'em!" I whispered as I flicked my thumb.

The rubber ball hurtled straight toward the elevator button. It bounced off the button with a *pop*, and the up arrow glowed orange.

"Bull's-eye!" I said.

"Nice!"

For once, Kei sounded excited. My heart pounded.

Come on, don't shout like that in my ear! You startled me!

"Why are you so quiet, Asuka?" Kei asked.

"N-no reason!"

I shook my head. After a minute or two, the elevator door opened.

"This is it. Focus," Kei ordered.

He was right—this was key. Unfortunately, the elevator had a camera inside. No matter what, I couldn't avoid being filmed. At first, I thought it would be better to take the stairs, but there are tons of cameras on the stairs, too, and no way to avoid them. According to Kei, they would capture my whole body from all different angles.

Apparently, Sawamoto had beefed up security since getting the Green Sea. He'd really gone out of his way to make my life hard! Otherwise, I could have raced up thirty flights of stairs in no time flat.

"I'm getting on," I said.

If I waited too long, the door would close, and all my work with the finger bomb would be for nothing. Scooping the rubber ball from the floor, I dived into the elevator. I pressed the button for the thirtieth floor right away and then stood in the back right corner. Kei had told me that that corner was directly below the camera.

The jacket and hat I borrowed (…okay, stole) were finally coming in handy. Since I was right below the camera, it would look like a guard was in the elevator. Count on Kei to think up something that clever.

The elevator closed, and it began to move silently up.

"Hey, Kei, we're not doing half bad," I said.

"The real test is ahead. Don't let your guard down. If anyone gets on the elevator, it's over," he answered.

That was true. Even if I'd fooled the security camera, I wouldn't be able to fool a real person. But Kei had thought of that, too, and confirmed that the guards only used the elevators when they changed shifts.

Meaning I was safe for a few moments.

"It's fine. You… Oh!" I broke off.

"What's wrong?"

The elevator had abruptly slowed down, and I was nowhere near the thirtieth floor.

"I think it's stopping! Someone's getting on!"

"What?! Hide!"

"Where?!"

I looked around in a panic. Where could I hide in a tiny elevator?

"Asuka, use your wristband!"

Seriously…?!

A second later, the elevator door opened with a *ding*.

"Huh? I thought I saw something just now…," the guard muttered, rubbing his eyes as he stepped into the elevator. "It's not fair, making me take over for someone just because they got a stomachache…"

I was looking down at him.

Using the special wire concealed in my wristband, I'd climbed out the service window on the ceiling of the elevator and was now on top of it. The window was sturdy and easy for me to lift.

The guard rode to the twenty-third floor without noticing me and got off.

"Whew, close call," I muttered.

"…Sorry. I didn't foresee that."

"It happens. No worries. He didn't see me."

"…"

Wait, he wasn't upset, was he?

"…This is fun."

"What?"

"It's exceedingly rare for any plan of mine to not go as I've calculated. This is the most fun I've ever had in my life!"

He was so excited, like a kid putting together a grand scheme. I didn't know he could sound like that…

Why was my heart pounding?

It must be because he was suddenly so out of character. That had to be it!

"Fun for you! I'm the one who's in here. Don't forget that, Kei!"

"Yeah, I know… Hey, why are you mad?"

"I'm not mad! Anyway, let's go get the Green Sea!!"

13

Face-to-Face with the Green Sea!

When the elevator got to the thirtieth floor, I dashed into the hallway. Glimpsing guards at the end of the passage, I pressed myself against a wall to hide. To my right was a big window and a sofa and table—probably a break area. To my left was the hallway.

"Hey, the elevator's open," one of the guards at the far end of the hallway said.

"The boss must be back," the other one said.

"But I don't see anyone…"

A flashlight beam lit up the wall, sweeping close to my face. I held my breath and stood absolutely still. I'd made it this far—I couldn't get caught now.

"You think something's glitched?"

I heard footsteps as a guard approached.

I flicked the red capsule in my fist.

Pop!

She collapsed to the floor.

"Hey, what happened?!"

The other guard came running.

Pop! Crash.

Kei's plan was unfolding with frightening accuracy.

I wrapped my scarf around my mouth and nose so I wouldn't breathe in the sleeping gas, then walked past the fallen guards down the hallway.

"I'm here. Is this the right place?" I asked Kei.

"*Yeah. Sawamoto's got the Green Sea hidden in his office at the end of this hallway. I know my intel is solid,*" he answered.

"Okay. I'm unlocking the door."

I took a small piece of wire from my belt. I'm good at picking locks; Dad made sure of that. Ten seconds later, there was a *click*, and the door swung open.

"*I see locks are useless against you, Asuka. I'll remember that,*" Kei said.

"Excuse me, I don't poke around in people's stuff. Everyone has things they don't want seen, and I'd never spy."

"*My secret stuff is highly complex. Even if you did see it, you wouldn't understand.*"

Come on! I said I didn't spy.

Kei snickered. Wait, was he teasing me?

"*Hurry up and go in. Someone might come.*"

"Got it."

I scanned the hallway for people, then went into the office.

"Wow, it's huge," I gasped.

The room was at least thirty feet across, with a big painting about six feet tall on the wall.

"Company presidents sure have big rooms," I said.

"It's over ten times as big as yours," he noted.

Why did he have to compare us? It was depressing. Also, he got one thing wrong.

"It's our room now," I corrected.

"…You're okay with that? I thought you didn't want me there," he said.

"That was ages ago. I forgot already."

"Hmm…your memory is worse than I realized."

Why was he like that? I just said something nice! And he had to ruin it!

"Get going. The last hurdle's ahead," he said, but I thought I heard a smile in his voice. I swear!

"Remind me to smack you later," I said.

Setting my complaints aside, I scanned the room. There was a massive wooden desk in the back left corner, with a puffy leather chair behind it. Behind that was a bookshelf.

"I bet that's it," Kei said.

"Yeah," I agreed. I pulled out a couple of books, and… "Bingo."

Behind the books was a panel of numbered buttons and a small display window.

"Good. Press the numbers I say."

I didn't even ask how he knew the combination. This was Kei, after all.

"…849214729341104937576358."

Okay, eight, four, nine, two…

Listening carefully so I wouldn't mess up, I pressed the numbers he said.

When I finished, there was a creaking sound, and the bookshelf split into two parts, which slid to the right and left.

"Wow, I've seen this in movies, but I didn't know it existed in real life!" I said.

"Forget the shelf—the Green Sea is what matters!"

"I know that."

Behind the shelf was a little door on what looked like a safe. It was glossy black, with a silver knob on the right side. I grabbed the knob and yanked. It was heavy, but little by little, the door opened.

"Whoa, there it is…!"

On the other side of the door was a small cushion, and on the cushion was a huge, glittering green diamond.

"Wow, it's beautiful!!" I gasped.

When I shone a light on it, the diamond glittered even brighter.

I'd never seen something so beautiful in my whole life!

"Stop ogling and get moving!" Kei snapped.

"Right…"

…Couldn't I ogle just a little?

That's the thing with something so gorgeous; you want to stare at it forever. Kei probably wouldn't understand, of course. I reached my hand toward the jewel.

"Boy am I nervous…"

I mean, it was worth three billion yen.

My hand started shaking at the thought, but I carefully picked it up and tucked it into my belt.

"Nice work. Now get out of—" Kei broke off.

"You! What are you doing?!" a voice shouted from the door.

My heart skipped a beat.

Busted?!

Spinning around, I saw a skinny middle-aged man with a narrow face. From where I was, I couldn't clearly make

out his expression. His flashlight was shining at me. I covered my eyes, but I could see his face between my fingers.

"It's him…," I murmured.

"Shuzou Sawamoto," Kei answered.

He was back! And I'd made it so far without being caught!

"You're a kid?! A little girl? Oh, never mind. What are you doing in here?"

He didn't seem to understand what was happening yet. Since I had my scarf over my face, he probably couldn't see my face well.

"K-Kei, what do I do?"

"Stay calm… You still have a gas capsule, right?" Kei's crisp voice in my ear kept my rising panic in check.

"Yeah," I answered.

But just as I reached into my belt to find the capsule, the beam of Sawamoto's flashlight glinted off the Green Sea.

"Hey! Why do you have…? Who are you?!" he thundered.

The cat was out of the bag.

"Who am I? Don't blame me if you can't handle the answer!"

"Asuka, wait!" Kei shouted frantically. But I didn't intend to stop.

I glared at Sawamoto, pointing at him. My right hand was on my hip. He looked at me in surprise.

"I am Phantom Thief Red, enemy of evil. I took the liberty of stealing the evidence of your crime!"

Oops, was that a bad idea?

"You didn't have to tell him who you were! And did you get that speech from a manga?" Kei shot back right on cue.

Okay, maybe. But if I'm doing this, I want to do it right! Next time, I think I'll come up with a special pose, just to show who's boss.

"You're Phantom Thief Red…?! A little girl like you…?! You're kidding."

"Nope."

He might not believe me, but he couldn't deny I'd suddenly shown up in his secret room. Quickly, he gathered his wits and hissed with frustration. "Where'd you hear about the Green Sea?!"

"You're a horrible person! I'm going to return the Green Sea to its rightful owner!" I retorted.

"Shut your mouth!!" Swinging the flashlight in the air, he lunged toward me.

"Eek!"

That came out of nowhere! I didn't have time to take out the gas capsule.

"Run!!" Kei screamed.

Sawamoto was right in front of me. The next instant—

"Wham!"

—I calmly threw out a punch that landed square on his solar plexus. He sank to the floor, unconscious.

"…Oh yeah, I forgot. You're not normal," Kei said.

Excuse me, that's not how you talk to people.

Although I had to admit, I wasn't weak enough to lose to that guy. He was a total beanpole.

"Sometimes, Dad and I spar," I said.

"That sounds like a fight between a bear and Bambi."

A bear and Bambi?

Well, Dad is almost six feet and jacked, so maybe he does look like a bear.

"Ever since I was little, Dad has let me challenge him to fights in exchange for my tough training routine. I worked really hard because I thought it would be amazing to beat a guy like him," I told Kei.

"You actually wanted *to fight him?! Your brain mystifies me."*

"Yours mystifies me. But lately, I've been giving Dad a run for his money. I'm starting to get to him."

"…Remind me never to get into a physical fight with you."

No worries there. I don't fight amateurs.

"Anyway, do you think the tussle just now tipped off the guards?" he asked.

I walked over to the door and listened. I didn't hear any alarms or footsteps.

"I think we're safe for now," I said.

"Okay," he said, then paused. *"By the way, Asuka, if they aren't on to you, then you still have ten minutes to make your escape according to the plan."*

"…What do you mean?"

I didn't know what he was getting at.

"Of course, you could leave the building right now…but you could also search for something…like a ring, for example."

No way! Did he mean…?

"B-but you said I wouldn't have time for that!"

"I always build in extra time. The break-in went so smoothly that you didn't need it."

"Wow…"

Wait, wait!

He should've told me that from the start! Then I wouldn't have said all those mean things!

"I thought you'd be distracted if I told you ahead of time. After all, Red's primary target is the Green Sea. But since you've achieved half of that mission, it's fine to pursue the secondary target…right?"

He sounded as calm as a grown-up.

"Kei…"

"You don't have much time, so if you want to do something, do it fast...and by the way, all the jewels other than the Green Sea should be hidden in the warehouse space one floor below you."

Wait, wait, what?!

He'd been planning to get the ring back all along! Otherwise, he wouldn't have found out where it was!

I may be a supergirl, but right now I wanted to cry.

14

Big Trouble!

I dashed out of the hidden room and took the elevator down one floor. The hallway was shorter than on the thirtieth floor, with two doors. I put my hand on the door to the right, but it was locked.

"Not again! I don't have time for this!"

I hurriedly picked the lock and stepped inside. It wasn't as big as Sawamoto's office, but it was still fairly large. About thirty shelves were lined up in neat rows covered with gemstones, paintings, and antiques.

"Whoa, I'm supposed to search all these?" I asked Kei.

There was no way I had time for that.

"Don't worry, you'll find the right shelf fast," Kei answered calmly.

"How?"

"Take a good look. The gems are organized by type, and the paintings and antiques are by value or year, right? There should be a turquoise section. If you walk around, you'll probably stumble across it."

Um, I don't think so. I could look all day and not figure it out...

"Kei, you look."

"Oh, fine."

I walked toward the back of the room, aiming my camera at the shelves. There were glittering rings, necklaces, and earrings. I wanted to stop and admire all of them.

"Keep going!" I told myself, shaking my head. I had to find the turquoise ring.

"Asuka, stop," Kei said when I reached a shelf in the middle of the room.

"Here?"

I turned to the shelf. There were about ten rings and pendants set with bright-blue stones on them.

"That appears to be the turquoise section," he said.

"Great, there's not too many!"

I took the certificate of authenticity with the picture of the ring out of my right arm pocket.

"You brought that? Then you must have been set on finding it from the start," Kei said.

"That's not t-true. I was planning to follow your instructions," I protested.

"Were you?" he said suspiciously.

I didn't have time to argue, so I started comparing the photo to the gems on the shelf. They all looked the same to me, but some of them weren't rings, so it shouldn't be too hard.

"…Not this one. Not this one, either. Close, but not quite. This one…is it!"

The blue of the stone seemed to float in the darkness. It was exactly like the photo. I compared them several more times. No question, this was it.

"Kei, I—"

Before I could finish, I heard the doorknob turn, and I darted into the shadow of the shelf.

The door swung open. It was Sawamoto. He was awake again—I should have hit him harder. Behind him was a guard so tall that his head practically bumped the ceiling.

"Not good," Kei said. I nodded.

There was only one way out. Since Sawamoto and the big guy were standing in front of it, I couldn't escape.

"I know you're in there! Come out!!" Sawamoto shouted. My body almost reflexively obeyed, but Kei stopped me.

"He's baiting you. Don't fall for it. Do you have the gas capsule?"

"Just one left. What do I do?"

One capsule wouldn't be enough to knock both of them out. On top of that, I wasn't sure how well it would work on such a big person.

"…Okay. We're getting you out."

"But don't you think they'll go away if I hide? They don't seem to know if I'm in here or not."

"I doubt that. They definitely know."

"How can you tell?"

He was the one who just said they were baiting me!

"They just don't know where you're hiding. This is the store-room. There's gotta be a security camera in here."

Oh…right.

No one would fill a room with jewels and other expensive stuff, then not put at least one security camera in it.

"Why didn't you tell me that? I ran in here all defenseless," I complained.

"I didn't foresee Sawamoto waking up. If he hadn't, you would've had plenty of time to escape," Kei answered.

"So what's your plan? You have one, right?"

He said he was getting me out, so he must have thought about how to do it.

"Of course. First…"

As I listened to his strategy, I peeked between the shelves at Sawamoto.

"You're not coming out? Fine, then we'll come to you!" he shouted.

The hulking guard headed toward me, squeezing uncomfortably into the cramped room. The shelf I was hiding behind was about fifty feet from the door. The guard approached with long strides, slowly checking each row.

"Now!" Kei hissed, and I hurled the gas capsule at the guard. It burst against the forehead of the unsuspecting big guy, and his knees collapsed to the ground with a *crash*.

"Now over here!" I muttered, flicking the rubber ball against the wall with my thumb.

It bounced off a wall near Sawamoto before hurtling into a big, tan vase. The vase tottered.

"That's worth seventy million yen!" Sawamoto screeched, propping it up.

Meanwhile, I shot from the shadow of the shelf toward the door. The big guy kneeled and shook his head like he was trying to chase away the drowsiness.

"Wait, that didn't knock him out? It's strong enough to work on a bear!" Kei shouted.

"Then he must be stronger than a bear!" I answered.

Still, he looked sleepy, and his movements were clumsy. I headed straight for him.

"Hey…you!"

His log-like arm reached out, but I pushed it away and leaped onto him.

"Here goes!"

Launching off his shoulder with one foot, I spun in mid-air before landing.

"Wait!!" Sawamoto shouted, still hugging the vase in both arms.

"Wait? Why would I wait?" I laughed. I waved good-bye as I burst into the hallway. "I should be able to get outta— Uh-oh!"

Guards were pouring out of the elevator. Their flashlights swept the hallway.

"I see they called their friends," Kei said.

"We don't have time for analysis, Kei!" I shouted.

"There's a staircase at the end of the hallway. Now's not the time to worry about cameras."

"Got it!"

I ran down the hallway, away from the guards, while they came thundering after me. They weren't as big as the guy in the storeroom, but they were all buff, like they did martial arts or something. Getting caught by one of them would be no joke.

When I got to the stairs, I leaped down four at a time. The guards were muscly, but that also meant they were clumsier, so I had an advantage in terms of speed. I shook them off in no time.

"I think I can get out now," I told Kei.

"Not so soon," he answered.

"Why not? The guards can't catch me."

"Can you hear that? Listen carefully."

"Huh?"

I froze and perked up my ears. I could hear multiple foot-steps approaching…from below! I ran to the next landing and leaned over it.

"I see 'er! Up there!" one of the guards shouted as our eyes met across about five flights of stairs. A bunch of them were running toward me.

"What do I do? I'm trapped!"

"…Go back to the floor above you and let them pass. It's a perfect spot."

"Why perfect?"

"Just talking to myself."

I was nervous, but I did as he said. I hadn't noticed on my way down, but this floor was a little different from the others. A few paces farther into the hallway was a big room with rows of tables and chairs. There was a counter, too, and bottles of soy sauce on the tables.

"Is this a cafeteria?" I asked.

"Yeah, the employee cafeteria. I think the next room is bet-ter. Go in there."

"The next room?"

I left the cafeteria and opened the door after it, and I immediately recognized it was a kitchen. There were silver stainless steel counters, a big refrigerator in the back, and a shelf full of seasonings I didn't recognize. I softly closed the door and crouched in the shadow of a counter.

"Whew…"

Even I was feeling a little tired. I know I'm strong, but being nervous and getting chased around takes a lot out of you.

"You okay? We need to revise our plan," Kei said.

"We do?"

"If you can stay here while they pass, great. But things might not go that well. Then what will you do?"

"What do you mean? The plan says I make my escape and expose Sawamoto's wrongdoing. I've got the evidence."

"...Is that enough for you?"

What was he getting at?

"We're doing better than I expected. Don't you agree?" he asked.

"I guess...?"

It was true that I'd expected us to make more mistakes on our first assignment. We'd even gotten Granny Yurie's ring back.

"When you make your escape, you'll probably have to tangle with some guards. Wouldn't it be quicker to just capture them all?"

"Uh...what? Wait a second! Are you serious?!"

Without thinking, I started to stand up.

He was right that I could probably beat a handful of guards in a head-on fight, but some of them were like that one guy who could shake off the gas.

"Of course, I don't expect you to fight them all. I'm talking about a trap."

"A trap?"

"Yeah. All you need to do is follow my instructions. I'll come up with the plan, like I always do."

Where the heck did that confident attitude come from?

Then again, who am I to talk?

I was bursting with excitement at the thought of a trap. After all, the good guys had to beat the bad guys!

"I'm in!" I told him.

"I thought you'd say that. Okay, so first…"

I could hear him smiling, and I started to do as he told me.

15

Phantom Thief Red in Their Element

"I know you're in here!"

The kitchen door slammed open as Sawamoto's voice boomed out.

The lights switched on.

I was hidden in the shadow of a stainless steel shelf, with a view of the door. On my back was a pack that had been tucked away in my clothes. You might wonder how that's possible, but all I can say is that it seemed to be compressed way down. I didn't even know it was there until Kei told me.

"Ready?" he asked.

"Ready," I answered.

I looked at the plastic water bottle and dry ice I'd taken from the garbage bin and refrigerator.

"Put the dry ice into the bottle. Don't close the lid yet," Kei instructed.

"Got it." I slipped several chunks of it into the bottle.

"No dice, eh? Then I'm coming in!!" Sawamoto thundered.

Just counting the ones I could see, there were four guards, including the big guy, plus Sawamoto. There could be more in the hallway.

"Okay. Close the lid and throw it."

I closed the lid and rolled it toward Sawamoto and the guards. It made it to their feet.

"Hey, what's this? …A water bottle? What's that about?" one of the guards snorted, raising his foot to stomp on it.

Just then—

Ka—boom!!

—the bottle blew apart.

"Oww!"

"What happened?"

"Calm down!"

"Something just hit me!"

The confused uproar of the guards filled the kitchen. Without waiting any longer, I threw the next plastic bottle I'd prepared.

"Another one!"

"Did that explosion come from this bottle?"

"It's gonna go off again!"

The guards backed away, all eyes on the bottle.

"Here's our moment. Go, Asuka!"

"Got it!"

Bursting out of the shadow, I broke the kitchen lights with a finger bomb, and the room went black. I switched to the infrared mode on my sunglasses. Two guards by the door were freaking out over the bottle. The rest appeared to have gone into the hallway.

"It's R-Red!!" one of them screamed, but I had already dashed into the hallway. About ten guards were out there.

Just as we'd planned.

"Well, well, look what we have here. Who'd have thought the famous Phantom Thief Red was so puny?"

Sawamoto was smiling wickedly, probably because his guards were surrounding me. The big guy was next to him.

"How do you know this is what I really look like? Maybe it's a disguise. Anyway, aren't you the one who left the room first?"

I made my voice low, like a grown-up, to make sure he didn't guess my real identity.

"What did you say?" He looked at me suspiciously.

"What's all the fuss? That's just an ordinary water bottle," I said, pointing to the second bottle I threw.

"You—!"

Sawamoto glowered at the guards. He was probably furious that they'd been tricked. Of course, I couldn't blame them when it was a plan Kei came up with. Even if they were adults.

"And how do you plan to escape now?" Sawamoto asked.

"How? …Like this."

I tightened the lid of the bottle in my hand and threw it at the guards.

"Ahh!" the guards shrieked, running from the bottle.

"You idiots!" the big guy shouted. "That was an ordinary water bottle in there! This one is—"

Ka—boom!

"Oww!"

"That was real!"

"Why are water bottles exploding?" The guards were running around the hallway in a frenzy.

"Don't let her escape!" Sawamoto roared.

"When did I say I was escaping?" I answered, gripping a walnut I found in the kitchen.

When the guards turned toward me, I started running

and flicked it at the ceiling. Bright-red powder rained from the plastic onto the guards.

"What is this…? Yeowww!"

"My eyes! My throat!"

Sawamoto and the other guards watched, stunned, as the guards with bright-red eyes and faces flailed around the hallway.

"Cayenne and habanero powder sure work fast," Kei said.

"Oooh, I bet that really hurts. You sure this is okay?" I asked.

It went so well, I was getting worried.

I hadn't been hiding in the kitchen doing nothing all that time. I could have escaped, but instead, I stayed to set Kei's trap.

I'd split open a plastic bag and stuck it on the ceiling. It was set up so that when the walnut hit it, half of it would come off. Getting the cayenne and habanero powder in there was hard, though. Even with a mask on and my scarf over that, my throat hurt.

"That sting could last for a couple days. The effects aren't per-manent, though," Kei said casually.

We were up against professional guards—we had to do something extreme to keep them from coming after me.

While they were flailing around, I ran down the hallway toward the stairs.

"Red's getting away! Follow them!" Sawamoto shouted, but the guards didn't listen.

After witnessing what happened to their coworkers, they probably figured it wasn't worth risking another trap.

Everything was going according to Kei's plan. In fact, it was going so well, it was like he knew what would happen from the start. Honestly, how does his brain work? Heck if I know.

Thanks to him, though, the guards hung back long enough for me to easily make it downstairs.

"We got the intel, so that was a success," Kei said.

"Yeah!" I agreed.

The "intel" was the number of guards. When we decided to catch them, we knew we needed that number. Kei had researched the building blueprint and location of the guards in advance, but we'd still run into trouble in the elevator.

To be safe, he said he needed to know the current number of guards. The reason I hid for so long in the kitchen was so they would all gather in one place and we could count them. Kei had sounded confident when he said that if Sawamoto knew I was hiding in there, he'd call all the guards. He was right, and he was also right about how I could get out.

"So how many guards are there?" I asked.

I'd been so busy following orders, I didn't have time to do the counting myself.

"According to my advance research, there should be fifteen in all. We knocked out three at the entrance and two in front of Sawamoto's room with sleeping gas, which should leave ten.

But there were twelve by the kitchen. That's two more than I thought."

"You think he called in backup?"

"Probably. Maybe because the Green Sea was here. Five went down from the pepper powder, leaving seven guards plus Sawamoto."

"Eight, huh? Including the big guy?"

I thought about those log-like arms.

"He's stuck to Sawamoto like glue, so unless we do something about him, we probably can't catch the boss. Did he look strong to you?"

"Yeah. I doubt he's stronger than Dad, but he's big, so he's got power and stamina. If he landed a hit on me, it wouldn't be good."

If possible, I wanted to avoid fighting him head-on.

"Don't worry, I'm not planning to put you in that position," Kei said.

"I hope not. By the way, I was wondering, why did the water bottles burst like that?"

When I stuffed the dry ice into the bottle and threw it, I hadn't expected it to make such a loud explosion.

"It's simple. When dry ice comes into contact with water, it produces what looks like white smoke. That's carbon dioxide. If the process occurs in a sealed bottle, the pressure from the carbon dioxide will blow up the bottle. That's what happened just now… Do you understand?"

"Uh…kind of."

Actually, I didn't, but I kept that to myself. I didn't have to understand the hard part. I just had to understand what would happen.

"No, you don't. I'll explain better later."

"That's okay."

Kei's explanations were so complicated, I usually got sleepy.

"Don't complain. Oh, this is your floor."

I stopped. The number 16 was written on the wall. Hiding in the shadows, I checked for guards before stepping into the hallway.

"This floor sure is messy," I said.

The hallway was littered with cardboard boxes and bits of metal. Considering the state of my room, I can hardly talk, but it looked a lot messier than the other floors.

"The nineteenth floor on down is occupied by Sawamoto's subsidiary companies. This one is a normal hundred-yen shop. The staff don't even know what Sawamoto is doing on the sly."

"A hundred-yen shop?"

A plate on one of the doors read HIKARI COMPANY. Hikari hundred-yen shops were famous around here. They were all over the place. Whenever I did any shopping there, they were always crowded.

"Sawamoto must be making plenty of honest money. Why does he deal in stolen goods?" I asked.

"The profits from a hundred-yen shop are nothing compared

with the profits from selling stolen goods. Also, he might have set up this company using money from his illegal business."

"Interesting. Meaning I don't have to feel bad. Oh, that's where I'm going?"

He'd just sent my target destination to my device. I went through the door with the plate and opened another door behind it. I was getting used to the way the locks just popped open.

"Ugh, what's in here? It's all dusty!"

I pulled my scarf over my mouth and nose. Steel shelves lined the walls, and there were cardboard boxes everywhere.

"A storeroom?" I asked.

"More like a closet. They've got other storerooms, so this is probably where they keep things temporarily and store sample items—stuff like that," he answered.

Still wouldn't hurt to clean it!

"Anyway, stay focused on the plan," Kei said.

"I am!" I snapped.

I was there to set the next trap. Although when Kei said he knew a good place to get equipment, I never guessed he meant a hundred-yen shop.

I opened a cardboard box at my feet. It was stuffed with random knickknacks: nylon string, scissors, packing tape, fishing line, and even cracker-ball fireworks. Maybe they were samples, like Kei said. I'd never seen those last two at my local hundred-yen shop.

"Fishing line and cracker balls. Hmm…," Kei said.

"Hmm" what?!

Kei already seemed to be cooking up some plan that I couldn't even imagine.

By the way, we'd decided if we were going to catch Sawamoto, we had to catch him unharmed. No matter how horrible a criminal he was, our work would be meaningless if we seriously injured him. It would damage the reputation of Phantom Thief Red, which Dad and Uncle K spent so much time building up, and that was the last thing I wanted. It was also one thing Kei and I agreed on. Although for him, it was more about proving there wasn't anything Uncle K could do that he couldn't.

"…Okay, I think we can work with this," he muttered after a long silence. Apparently, his plan was complete.

"Asuka."

"What?" I asked expectantly.

"I've got it. All you need to do is follow my instructions."

As usual, his voice was bursting with confidence.

16

Time to Turn the Tables!

Following Kei's directions, I stuffed what we needed into my backpack and returned to the hallway.

That's when I made a mistake.

Everything had gone so well until then, I think I assumed the guards hadn't caught up with me.

"Red!"

No sooner had I stepped into the hallway than someone grabbed my left arm. They pulled it so hard that I almost lost my balance, but I managed to stay standing.

I turned around. It was a guard, but it wasn't the big guy. That was a relief. I glanced around. I didn't see any more guards. This one must have found me by chance.

"Asuka!" Kei shouted.

"I'm fine," I answered calmly.

"'You're fine'? Mighty relaxed for someone who just got caught. Hmph, what a scrawny arm. You're as puny as a kid!" the guard said.

She tilted her head like she was puzzled. She must have gotten distracted by how skinny my arm was, because she

left herself wide-open. I dived toward her chest.

"Whoa!" For a second, the guard froze in surprise.

"'Caught'?" I said, pushing up the hand that was grasping my left arm and grabbing her wrist with my right hand. "You can't catch me that easily!"

I yanked her arm straight down.

"Urgh!" she groaned.

She flipped over onto the floor with a *thud*, and she didn't show any sign of standing up again. I cautiously walked up to her. She was unconscious.

"*…Was that aikido?*" Kei asked, sounding impressed.

"Yeah. Dad taught me there are certain moves where strength doesn't matter."

I tied the guard's hands behind her back, covered

her mouth with packing tape, and pushed her into the closet. Even if she woke up, she'd have a hard time calling the other guards.

"That cost us some time. We better hurry... Ouch."

I started to run—then grimaced as pain shot through my left arm.

"Hey, are you okay?" Kei asked.

"Um, yeah. I guess that guard hurt my arm a little when she pulled it...but I'm not left-handed, so it's fine."

"I hope so...but tell me if it gets worse."

"Thanks. I'm fine, I promise."

I rotated my left arm a few times, then started running again. My elbow felt hot. I knew that wasn't good, but I didn't want to whine to Kei after he'd done such a good job guiding me.

This wasn't enough to stop me. We'd come so far. I wanted to finish it off.

I finally reached the first floor. There was the tasteless bronze statue, still standing there in the big entryway. I felt like ages had passed since I was last there, but when I glanced at the clock, I saw it had only been around two hours.

The only people left standing were Sawamoto and six guards. The exit was right in front of me, but of course I didn't run for it. I planned to set the final trap before I left.

"That's a good spot. Is the fishing line okay?"

"Yeah, I checked it. Now I just wait, right?"

"Yeah. If you follow the plan, it'll be over in seconds."

Every time I bent my left arm, I grimaced with pain. I was glad Kei couldn't see my face. If he could, I'm sure he would have canceled the plan.

I took a deep breath and looked up.

I could hear someone running down the stairs.

"The game ends here, Red!!" someone shouted.

"Finally. This was a wild-goose chase…"

Sawamoto and the guards emerged from the stairwell, dripping with sweat. They must have searched the other floors top to bottom. I guess throwing cracker balls at the security cameras in the stairwell to cover the lenses in scratches and soot was a good idea after all.

"Looks like your luck ran out. Just a few more feet, and you'd have been out the door!" Sawamoto smirked.

Apparently, catching up with me had restored his smugness. Just like Kei predicted. He and his guards didn't have the slightest idea I'd been waiting there to ambush them. They thought they'd caught me right as I was trying to slip out the front door.

"True, but it's not over yet," I said, backing away.

"Oh, no you don't!"

The guards worked together to surround me with well-practiced skill. I casually noted their positions.

"Great spot," Kei said through the earphones.

Sawamoto and the big guy were standing right in front of

me. Their faces were bright red, maybe because they were so mad about the wild-goose chase. I could tell the other guards were bloodthirsty, too. Even I couldn't take on this many of them at once. My arm was hurting bad enough that fighting even one of them could be rough. I bit my lip.

"Here I go," I told Kei.

"Go for it!"

I hurled the rest of the cracker balls concealed in my hand against the floor. They crackled and spat.

"Watch out, it's a bluff!! Don't let a brat like that beat this many of us!" the big guy hollered, but I still had a moment's opening. That was plenty. I shot a wire toward the ceiling.

"Catch 'em!"

As one of the guards lunged toward me, I flicked a walnut at him.

"!"

It hit his forehead, stopping him short. By then, the wire was pulling me into the air. I ended up about five feet below the ceiling, which, in the entryway, was two floors high.

"Now what do you plan to do? There's nowhere left to run!" Sawamoto sneered, looking up at me.

Obviously, I wasn't trying to escape.

I pulled the fishing line that had been in my left hand the whole time until it was taut. It was attached to the statue of Sawamoto. From below, they shouldn't be able to see it— and they were directly below the statue.

Kei's plan was simple. Knock the statue over on top of them.

To capture the remaining guards and Sawamoto all at once, we needed something big. He had calculated where Sawamoto, his guards, and I would be standing when they surrounded me during my escape attempt. We could catch them unawares, since they probably wouldn't expect a statue to fall on them.

I yanked the fishing line as hard as I could.

"Ouch!"

Pain tingled in my left arm, but I didn't let up.

Obviously, the statue didn't budge just from that. But my body began swinging like a pendulum.

"What's Red up to?"

Sawamoto and the guards stared blankly up at me.

"If you take too long, they might move. You've gotta get it the first time," Kei reminded me.

"I know!"

I swung toward the wall and kicked off with both feet as hard as I could. I was aiming for one point: the statue's head. Normally, I could never knock over something that was fifteen feet tall and weighed over six hundred pounds. But the statue's center of gravity was the base. The top part was light. Kei had calculated that if I pushed the head, I could knock the whole thing over.

I believed in that prediction.

I believed in Kei.

"Gooooooooooooo!!" I shouted as my feet landed on the statue's face. The force of the blow vibrated through my whole body, but I kicked as hard as I could.

"You think you can knock over...? Ahhhh!"

Sawamoto and the guards were staring wide-eyed.

The statue tottered, then fell straight toward them.

Booooom!!

The room shook, and dust swirled. Guess no one's been cleaning the statue. I sure wouldn't want to.

"*Cough, cough...* Wow, that's a lotta dust. But that went well!" I said to Kei.

"*Of course it did... I planned it,*" he answered.

The guy has no modesty. That's Kei, though.

"Did anyone get hurt?" I asked, lowering myself to the floor on the wire.

I didn't notice any sign of life under the statue.

"*It has a lot of mass, but most of it is in the base. The rest isn't heavy enough to kill anyone.*"

"I'm amazed it really fell. I mean, it's over six hundred pounds. Who'd have thought you could kick something like that over?"

"*You probably think that because it's a bronze statue. Imagine it was something smaller. Like a can of soda on a flat table with only a quarter of the soda left. If you wanted to push it over with one finger, where would you push?*"

"Um, the top? I don't think it would fall if you pushed the bottom."

"*Right. A bronze statue is a big version of that. Of course, it's* much *bigger; you had to push pretty hard. I figured your ridiculous strength would do the job if it was magnified by a pendulum.*"

"Uh, can you not call my strength ridiculous…?"

Who did he think he was anyway?

"*Asuka!*" he said out of nowhere.

"…What?" I answered sulkily.

"*Look at the statue! Quick!!*"

"Huh?"

He sounded really worried, so I spun around.

"You're kidding…!" I could hardly believe what I was seeing.

The statue was rising into the air. Slowly, the big guy appeared from under it, lifting the statue with one hand. He was insanely strong.

His clothes were dusty and torn in places. I'd hurt him, but clearly not enough.

"…Nice work," Sawamoto said.

Just then, the statue fell back to its original position with a *crash*. Apparently, the big guy didn't plan to rescue Sawamoto or the other guards. "You won't get away with this!!" he bellowed.

His eyes were bloodshot— Oh, he was raging mad now.

"What do I do? I think he's hurt, so maybe I can…"

"*Asuka, no. Just run,*" Kei interrupted.

"What are you saying?!" I was confused.

"I know your left arm is badly hurt. There's no way you can fight that colossus right now! You've done plenty. Get out of there, and fast!"

He'd noticed...

...but he'd stayed quiet long enough to let me carry out the plan.

Maybe Kei's not so bad after all.

Still...

"...No, Kei," I said flatly.

"What are you saying? I said you've done enough!" he shouted.

"It was my fault I got hurt. I'm not backing down."

I looked the big guy right in the eye. I was much faster than him, so I bet I could confuse him. He was also swaying a little on his feet, maybe from the statue blow. I stepped toward him.

"Asuka, no!"

I heard Kei, but I ignored him.

When the big guy saw me approaching, he swung his log-like arm. I planted my foot and leaped to the left. Thanks to the blow from the statue, the big guy seemed weak, staggering from the force of his own swing.

This was my chance!

Circling behind him, I kicked the back of his knees. He reeled.

"It's working!" I crowed.

"No, Asuka, it's a trap!" Kei said.

Huh?

My arms reached up reflexively to guard my head, and the big guy's hand slammed down on top of mine.

"Ahh!"

I flew backward. Unable to catch myself, I sprawled on the floor.

"Hey, you okay?"

"...Uh, I think so... Oof!" I tried to sit up, but sharp pain shot through my left arm. I grimaced.

"That's enough. Run!" Kei said.

"I want to, but I think it's too late," I said.

When I looked up, the big guy was bearing down on me. The stumbling and reeling had been an act. I shouldn't have been so stubborn. I should've listened to Kei.

"Sorry...I know you're always right...," I said.

"Stop apologizing, you idiot! We can't let Phantom Thief Red lose! Can you shoot a wire?"

"Yeah..."

"I'll tell you when. Aim at the ceiling and get up there as fast as you can!"

"I don't think going up will—"

"Just do it!"

He was so intense about it that I stopped arguing. All I could do was trust him.

The big guy clumped toward me while I was still sitting on the ground. When he got close, I could see his muscles were as hard as rock. No way could I bring him down.

"Tired of running, are we? I never guessed Red was a scrawny brat like you…," the big guy said.

I didn't answer.

"It's over," he said, reaching toward me.

"Now!" Kei said.

I shot the wire at the ceiling. My body rose into the air.

"Hey!" The big guy leaned back, dodging the wire right in front of his face.

"Too bad—," he said, starting to smile.

"Take that!"

But I kneed him right in the chin.

His head flew up, and he staggered back two or three steps before falling onto his butt.

"…You…"

He started to stand up, but then he collapsed onto his back, legs outstretched. He made no sign of getting up.

"What's going on…?"

I couldn't believe my eyes. Why had one blow from my knee knocked him out?

"You hit him in the chin. No matter how tough someone is, a strong blow to the chin will shake their brain. When that happens, the body cuts off nerves to the brain to protect it. Then the body doesn't work how it's supposed to. It's called a concussion. If the blow is strong enough, it can knock someone out, like what just happened. I didn't want to let you do it because it's dangerous, but I'm glad it worked."

"Ha-ha-ha. Yeah, I'm glad, too."

I could only laugh weakly. My knees were shaking. This was totally different from fighting Dad. To tell the truth, I was fighting for my life.

It was terrifying—but I won.

"No point hanging around. Let's get going," Kei said.

"Yeah," I agreed.

I unsteadily pulled my heavy body up from the ground.

After tying up Sawamoto and the guards, I stepped quietly outside. It was still dark, and I could hear the siren of a police car in the distance.

I looked up at the building. I'd left a card reading, *Phantom Thief Red was here!* next to Sawamoto. I'd set the Green Sea beside him, too, so he couldn't argue his way out of this. Dad and Uncle K had said they'd return the diamond to its rightful owner themselves, but according to Kei, it would eventually reach the owner if we gave it to the police, too. They'd just have to wait a little longer.

"Stop spacing out, Asuka. Don't get yourself arrested," Kei said.

"I'm going now."

I turned away from the building and ducked down the alley where my clothes were hidden. After quickly changing, I went back to the main street.

The police had arrived, and I could see the colored lights reflecting on the walls.

"Hey, kid, what are you doing here?" someone said.

I flinched. Turning around timidly, I came face-to-face with a middle-aged policeman eyeing me suspiciously.

"Um, just taking a walk."

"At this time of night?" Yeah, he didn't believe me.

Of course this had to happen!

How ridiculous would it be if we managed to accomplish the whole mission, only to be caught on the street?

"Um, tests are coming up! I stayed up late studying, and I was just getting a little fresh air."

"Studying for tests, huh? I see."

His expression softened, and the tension drained from my shoulders. He seemed to believe me.

"Did something happen over there?" I asked.

"It's nothing to worry your little head over. Run along home now," he said.

"Yes, sir."

I continued casually down the street. I felt him watching me, but I didn't look back. It was fine. No one would guess Red was an elementary schooler. Forcing myself to stay calm, I kept walking for a while. Turning a corner, I saw a familiar face.

"Kei!" I ran up to him.

"Good work," he mumbled.

No expression, no enthusiasm, no emotion on his face. Huh? Regular old Kei was back. Well, Red's work was over—but I wished he would stay like he was earlier.

"…How's your arm?" he asked, glancing at the one I'd hurt.

"It's fine. I think I twisted it a little. There might be a bruise where I guarded against the big guy's punch."

"…Sorry."

"Why? That I got hurt? It was my fault. Don't worry about it."

That was a surprise. I didn't know how to handle an apology from Kei.

"If I'd made a better plan, he wouldn't have gotten you."

Really? I don't think even Kei could have prevented that. He really was a perfectionist.

"But we did it. Our first job as Phantom Thief Red!" I said.

"Yeah, although we did run into a lot of trouble."

"We have one more thing to do before the sun comes up. Come with me, Kei."

"...You sure like to stick your nose in other people's business," he groaned.

Still, maybe I was imagining it, but his tone sounded a little softer than usual.

Was I hearing things? Or maybe...

I glanced at him. Nope—still no expression.

Epilogue

"So Granny Yurie got her ring back?" I asked.

I was lying on my bed, talking to Misaki on the phone.

"She said it was sitting in her entryway this morning, wrapped in some red fabric that looked like a scarf. She had no idea where it came from, and neither does anyone else. But it would be strange to take something to the police that was yours in the first place."

"I wouldn't worry about that. The important thing is, she got the ring back."

"Easy for you to say. It's just *weird*. Who do you think put it there?"

"Maybe it was a nice thief who sticks their nose in other people's business," I suggested.

"What are you talking about?"

"Who knows? Anyway, I've gotta go."

"What? Wait a minute!"

She sounded like she wanted to say something, but I hung up on her and yawned. On the way back from Sawamoto's building, Kei and I had dropped the ring off at Granny

Yurie's house and then walked home. I slept for five hours, but I was still dead on my feet.

"Asuka, they're talking about Sawamoto on TV," Kei said from in front of his computer.

"Seriously?!"

"Look."

He showed me the video on his computer. In the middle of the screen was a female reporter holding a microphone and standing a slight distance from the building as she gave an excited report.

"Red has struck again, here in our backyard! This is the very building visited by our resident phantom thief! It seems this is where the criminal suspect Sawamoto was selling stolen goods, including the Green Sea, a diamond worth three billion yen that had been stolen last month overseas. Red traced him here and then stole the diamond back.

"When the police arrived at the building, they found Sawamoto with the Green Sea and Phantom Thief Red's calling card next to him. Red appears to have left the diamond as evidence of Sawamoto's crime. The police plan to return the Green Sea to its owner as soon as their investigation is over.

"According to a source associated with the investigation, the police intend to pursue Sawamoto's trade criminal network as well as the whereabouts of Phantom Thief Red."

The shot shifted from the reporter to the TV studio. Kei turned his screen back toward him.

"They're after us," I said.

"That's how it goes. We're Phantom Thief Red," he answered. I burst out laughing. For once, Kei's eyes were twinkling a little.

"Thanks for everything, Kei," I said, looking out the window.

"…Why so grateful all of a sudden?" he asked.

"You got me out of some tight spots." I couldn't even count how many.

"…No problem. We're doing this Red thing together," he said brusquely.

Huh, so he felt that way, too. Well, then I was confident we could keep going.

Kei was still facing his computer, so I turned toward his back.

"Let's keep it up, partner," I whispered.

Afterword

Hi there.

I know it's a sudden question, but have you ever wanted to be a phantom thief?

I have.

When I was younger, I wanted to be either a phantom thief or an ace detective.

To make sure I was ready, I broadened my knowledge by reading the newspaper from front to back and observing people all over town. But whenever I decided one of those people must be carrying something dangerous and followed them, they always turned out to be an ordinary shopkeeper or something...

Clearly, I didn't have what it took to be either. What a disappointment.

But I didn't let that stop me. Maybe I could write stories! I mean, Lupin and Kid were storybook characters anyway. If I became the recorder of their adventures, I could watch phantom thieves from a closer range than anyone else!

That was when Asuka and Kei popped into my head.

At first, I wasn't sure elementary schoolers could be phantom thieves, but Asuka and Kei had some really incredible powers. I sure did worry about them, though. Asuka was always jumping into trouble, and Kei never stopped staring at his computer with that poker face. Would they be okay?

(If only they knew what it's like to keep an eye on them!)

But eventually, they made a break for it.

I was as surprised as you.

…Hey, is that Asuka making a peace sign like she owns the world? Sheesh, one compliment, and there they go.

Asuka and Kei are still new at all this, though, so I hope you'll be cheering for them.

Speaking of which, I hope you'll be cheering for me, too, as their recordkeeper. ☺

One last thing. Asuka did a lot of dangerous and violent things in this book. Please do not copy her under any circumstances. They only got away with it because Asuka trains all the time and Kei knows everything.

I can't wait to see you when their story continues!

Shin Akigi